Awaiting Grace

Awaiting Grace

Rosanne Daryl Thomas

Picador USA   New York

Picador® is a U.S. registered trademark and is used by St. Martin's Press under license from Pan Books Limited.

Design by James Sinclair

Library of Congress Cataloging-in-Publication Data

Thomas, Rosanne Daryl.
    Awaiting grace / Rosanne Daryl Thomas. — 1st ed.
        p.   cm.
    ISBN 0-312-20275-X
    I. Title.
PS3566.P575A56   1999
813'.54—dc21   99-21856
                                                            CIP

First Edition: June 1999

10   9   8   7   6   5   4   3   2   1

For
August Siena Cohn-Thomas
and her godmother,
Joanna Edwina Doreen Knatchbull,
with love

"Do you believe in Magic?" asked Colin, after he had explained about Indian fakirs. "I do hope you do."

"That I do, lad," she answered. "I never knowed it by that name, but what does th' name matter? I warrant they call it a different name i' France an' a different one i' Germany. Th' same thing as set th' seeds swellin' an' th' sun shinin' made thee a well lad an' it's th' Good Thing. It isn't like us poor fools as think it matters if us is called out of our names. Th' Big Good Thing doesn't stop to worrit, bless thee. It goes on makin' worlds by th' million—worlds like us. Never thee stop believin' in th' Big Good Thing an' knowin' th' world's full of it—an' call it what tha' likes."

—Frances Hodgson Burnett

Awaiting Grace

Being what You would most probably identify as a god, or God, depending upon your point of view, I am often tired at the end of the day and want nothing more than to enfold myself in the great and glittering nothingness, or everythingness, again depending on your point of view, of the all-changing eternal.

Nonetheless, I know your circumstances are difficult at best. You are ceaselessly vain, but at times I bear more fondness for You than You do for yourselves. This may be my own bit of pride. For I see the divinity within You and honor that by employing the capital letter that connotes the divine in your languages. And yet, You separate yourself from Me and mine. You prefer, perhaps out of modesty or fear—embracing the divine in oneself leads to more mystery than certainty—to use the lowercase, spurning the spark and the implications of that big Y. Never mind. I shall not quibble. In this instance, I defer to your mortal conventions to avoid the distraction of a fuss. I know you feel burdened and do not need additional worry. More than the most excruciatingly rare and delicate members of Creation, humankind seems to need constant tending and care. Certainly more than I am inclined to give. I've never been much of a nurturer in the conventional sense. Even so, from time to time for my own reasons, which, for all you know, may be either idle ones or important beyond human comprehension, I find myself taking a rather direct interest in certain individuals.

Sheila Jericault was one of these.

Sheila was blessed with eyes that matched a clear sky on an autumn day, and with wavy hair, reddish gold, that shot sunlight back to the sun. Sheila was comely enough to count her looks among her advantages. She was not what you would call a saint, and I've seen worse sinners. Those are human values anyway, and I don't wish to distract myself with such fluid matters at present. What interested *me* about Miss Sheila Jericault was her soul.

Poor Sheila had lost it.

It's a common problem, but for reasons that will ultimately become clear to you or not, as you wish, Sheila caught my eye. Like many a mortal, Sheila Jericault did not remember when or how she'd lost her soul. Her attention was elsewhere. But she did know exactly when she discovered it missing.

We'll get to that.

At thirty, Sheila Jericault was still unaware of her loss, and rather than feeling barren in spirit, she was feeling gleeful and godlike, particularly within her sphere. Without the slightest humility or doubt, Sheila believed she was orchestrating a minor miracle within the world of politics, which was, at the time, the world she cared most about.

A decent and likable Episcopalian named Ed Gilman had served his district as Representative for as long as anyone cared to remember. Everyone loved him and voted for him every two years and that was that, and that was just fine.

Until Sheila and until the candidate upon whose behalf

Sheila's personal miracle was being worked: Kip Coxx. Kip Coxx matters to my story, and perhaps to you yourself in the exceedingly grand and interconnected scheme of things, and thus you ought to know a bit about him. Mr. Kip Coxx was one of those men best defined by what he wanted. For instance: He was a lawyer turned real estate developer who wanted to win a congressional seat. Why? Because he wanted to. Kip also wanted a pretty wife who would be undemandingly devoted and helpful to him in his career. Early on, he found such a woman in the former Miss Polly Fayerweather. Mrs. Polly Coxx was an ideal candidate's wife, pretty enough to be quite pleasing but not pretty enough to alienate the voters who were not themselves possessed of inspiring pulchritude. She'd never had any tricky business dealings and she kept her opinions to herself, so no one had any easy reason to think ill of her. Yet. Polly and Kip had freckle-faced twin boys, Kippy Junior and Chip. The boys were polite and photogenic and knew how to keep reasonably clean without looking like sissies. And thanks to nature's extraordinary timing, Kip had even more going his way. On July Fourth Polly had gone into an early labor and pushed a third son into the world in time for the evening news: George Washington Coxx.

You might think that Kip was especially blessed by me or one of my ilk, but he wasn't. We, and I think I can speak for most of my colleagues in this instance, are almost entirely indifferent to politicians and scornful of those who presume to speak in our various names. If Coxx was blessed at all, he was blessed by luck and Sheila Jericault.

Sheila's job as Kip's campaign manager was to take this ambitious piece of flesh and mold him into a viable candidate. As I have said, she was aware that she had done a fine job. She wasn't the only one who considered her artistry more than a nifty feat. She was proud of her idea to make it a major campaign point that Coxx spoke for himself. Loudly, he decried spokesmen and handlers and the usual political rigmarole. Voters liked him for it because they wanted to believe a man could be all his own man and still run for office and win. Sheila knew that was a fairy tale, but she didn't care as long as voters believed it. Just as his phony independence was her idea, so was her own discretion. So often strategists not only ran the show, they were the show. Sheila avoided all that and worked at invisibility, the better—as a godlet, or faux-god, if you wish—to illuminate the artificial creation she called The Real Kip Coxx. Officially, only Coxx spoke for Coxx. Unofficially, it was Sheila who put the words in his mouth and, for the umpteen-millionth time in the history of politics, coined Coxx's slogan: Time for a change.

And what a gem that was. "Time for a change," Kip said on the radio. "Time for a change," he said on the stump. "Time for a change," he said on TV as, young and tanned, a vision of possibility, he stood beside Polly and Kippy, Chip, and chubby-cheeked, pink, and smooth baby George, who could not tell a lie. "Time for a change. Time for a change," he said, holding George and a fluffy white diaper as he reeled in the women's vote. "Time for a change," he said, and he said it a lot. And although Ed Gilman's contented constituents had no strong reason or desire to contemplate changing something that worked so wonderfully well for so many, Sheila's magic words had been spoken.

And the spell took.

Soon, for no tangible reason, the public seemed to agree that yes, indeed, it was time for a change. Reaching for the nearest thing, as humans are apt to do, they came to believe that Kip Coxx was just the man to bring this desirable yet undefined change about. And, in a peculiar way, he was. Just not at all in the way Sheila, much less the public, or humankind as I prefer to call them, expected.

A Hint

It is often said that my ways are mysterious. But let it not be said that I led you blind. At least not entirely. At least not this once. I'll give you a hint in the hope that it is of some use to you:

Consider all the miracles or might-be miracles of which you have heard (never mind the ones that are undefined, unnoticed, unacknowledged, refuted, or ignored). Now consider the path of those whose lives intersect with the miraculous.

Is it possible to expect that one might stride through time with a steady, majestic gait—heart untroubled and motive pure—until one is in the predestined place and standing nose-to-nose with the wonder of the divine made miraculously manifest to man?

Or are miracles to be stumbled upon?

Is the road neatly drawn in red on the map? Is this path straight, well lit, and clearly marked?

Or is the road to miracles the unsketched, unlikely, not necessarily inevitable or compelling choice, often lovely, just as often unlovely, bumpy, higgledy-piggledy, poorly marked, and regularly blocked?

From my point of view, the answer is: Yes.

I'm sure you see it differently. And you are absolutely right.

Now I return to Sheila and her soul.

Some Things About Sheila

S ome people can witness and endure all the worst that man can do and still, somehow, love. Others can bear only a modest amount of heartbreak before faith of any kind becomes too hard to have, especially faith in love. Sheila was one of the fragile ones, with a chipped porcelain teacup of a heart. Having such a heart, Sheila had decided some time ago that it was best not to use it. Heat, cold, a careless gesture, and it might shatter altogether. And then there was all that gluing to be done. What a mess. What a bother. It only made trouble.

As far as Sheila was concerned, Mr. Hal Orinsek had taught her that lesson and a lot of things she might have wished she didn't know, and though you might think this would make him a man to be avoided, Sheila did not. They were not enemies. They were not estranged. In spite of, or perhaps because of, the pain he had once caused her, his praise mattered more than any other praise, and Sheila could barely wait for his arrival and her due.

Sheila stood beside Polly Coxx on this glorious, warm October day admiring what she saw: glorious, happy voters eating glorious burgers hand-flipped by the candidate and splendid, glorious pies home-baked by Polly. "Glorious," she said to Polly.

Polly jostled her round-cheeked little baby. "Yeah," she said and stared off somewhere.

Sheila looked at her watch and thought again of Hal. "Little George looks just like a Buddha," she said to the candidate's wife, feeling the need to bring Polly back.

Polly returned from wherever her thoughts had taken her. "Do you know that if he were, if little Georgie were, I'd be a goddess? My womb would be a shrine. Isn't that lovely?" Polly fluffed her hair as if to show how a goddess might do it, a goddess with straight, dirty-blond hair and an upturned nose.

"Not bad," murmured Sheila, seeking out the candidate with her eyes. Kip was wearing his barbecue apron, flipping burgers, shaking hands, and laughing. He was doing fine.

"Except."

"Except what?" Sheila asked idly.

"I'd be dead."

"For chrissake."

"Well, that's what I heard. When the Buddha died, I mean the number-one one, his mom died seven days after. But it'd kill me to die and not raise my kids. Even if I got to be a goddess in the bargain."

Jesus H. Christ! thought Sheila, alarmed at her own alarm, but what she said was, "Where in the world do you pick up these things?" And then, because she had no wish to chat about Buddhas and dying and kids either with or without mothers when there were things to be done and an election to be won, she said, "Look at this. Straight out of a brochure. Come see autumn in Connecticut. Who else but your husband could plan an outdoor fund-raiser this late in the year? Even nature is on his side."

"Yeah," Polly sighed. "You don't have to tell me. Do you realize I used only fresh apples grown in the district?"

"You *are* a goddess," said Sheila, blowing baby George a kiss. She raced over to Kip and whispered in his ear.

"May I have your attention?" shouted the candidate, tapping three times with his spatula. "Ladies and gentlemen, a moment please!" Sheila discreetly held up one finger until she felt the crowd had quieted sufficiently, then she touched her mouth and Kip began to speak. "I would like to announce that every apple in today's delicious homemade apple pies—which, as you probably know, were baked by my incredible wife, Polly—every apple in Polly's pies tells the story of the hardworking men and women here in our great district! Winesaps from over at Bell's orchard in Westington, Romes from the fine Stone family here in Fallowfield; Stewart's out by Farbury Falls supplied the tart Granny Smiths. And wouldn't you say we're all proud to bursting of the mouth-watering fruits of their labors?"

There was a great cheer and a breeze blew through the state flag, causing it and the red, white, and blue to unfurl with a snap.

Sheila saw the air-slapping flags as a good sign because that's what she wanted it to be. She ignored the sign she'd been given, quite generously, by those like myself who are intermittently concerned with human affairs. But then, it seems that is what most people do most of the time. Before the breeze settled and the flags went limp, she was in her car on the way to Fallowfield Station to meet the 2:47. Damn, she thought. She'd forgotten to eat and yearned for a piece of Polly's pie. No doubt it would have been perfect. The best she'd ever tasted. Damn. She drove and she rummaged in her purse for her LifeSavers. Without looking at the colors, she shoved three in her mouth and crunched. The LifeSavers didn't satisfy. They didn't satisfy, but she needed them if she wasn't going to smoke, and there was no time to get more. Damn. No time. No time for anything except the next thing. No Buddhas no babies no heartbreaks no pain—just victory in two glorious weeks and that was all, period.

Hal's train had been early. He was pacing the platform. Sheila tapped on her horn and waved. Hal refused to move. "Okay. You win," she muttered amiably as she got out of the car. This was a game they'd played before. She expected it. She stepped up on tiptoe to kiss his cheek, but he turned his head and met her mouth with his own. "Damn it, Hal," she said, but she did not break away. If she couldn't have apple pie, she'd have this. A little snack.

"You taste like cherry," he said.

"And you are very, very naughty. That was all. That was it. No more nonsense. Okay?"

"Did I tell you I'm engaged?" Hal said.

"To a wonderful heck-of-a-fine gal with shitloads of money. Am I right?" Sheila didn't pause for an answer. She had no use for the details. "Thank God," she said, not referring to me. "You'll have to behave."

But Hal was one of those men who never had to behave. He just had to be discreet. And clever, which he was by nature. Did I mention that Sheila had loved him? Four years before. I wasn't paying attention, but from what I gather, Hal had been so charmed by the innocence of her affection that he was practically faithful for six months or so, but Hal was Hal. As I told you, from her point of view it was he who, in his careless way, had coaxed Sheila toward cynicism, convincing her that life would be best lived without a heart. He did not have one, though she'd heard it beat. He had no heart and he was happy, she had a heart and she was heartbroken, so she concluded that hearts were best not had. She dried her tears. And learned from Hal. Once she got used to the empty place inside her chest, she forgot about her heart and the horrible inconvenience it had been. So what? she thought, and after a bit of practice, she liked that. Not caring was grand and painless. Now and then she might feel a tug or a tingle, as she might have done if she were an amputee confused by a phantom limb. But not often. And she could get past those moments simply by getting busy.

Were it not for Hal, perhaps her heart might have remained a usable vessel. Perhaps not, for she herself was the one inclined to treat it in this way. In any case, were it not for Hal, Sheila would most certainly never have been enjoying success as a canny political strategist. She had not studied *The Art of War*. She was not a passionate partisan. She'd never stood in the autumn wind handing leaflets to people who were only half likely to vote at all. She hadn't put in her time or paid her dues or any of those things. She was just extraordinarily good at figuring out what to do. Not with her own life. Dear me. Not at all. The mortal known in this life as Sheila Jericault preferred to pretend she didn't have one. She would giggle with something like pride or relief and say, "I don't have a life," which I, whom many humans would define as immortal (who can say?), found irksome in the extreme, to the point where now and again I'd feel the temptation to take it away simply in my own irritation at her wastefulness. How many people who genuinely don't have lives might like them back? But never mind. All I wanted to say was that Sheila was good at figuring out what the next line (and better still, the next few lines after that) would be in the unwritten play of political theater. And that was a valuable knack. Hal Orinsek knew it. He had it, too. Only he was famous for it, and rich. People paid big for that knack. Not people, exactly. Politicians. Paid plenty. And if you are not going to have a heart, money is especially nice. Four years ago, Sheila had watched Hal do what he did so well, and just for the fun, she'd joined in. When Hal saw how often Sheila knew exactly what his client should be saying next, and how he should say it and when, he gave up trying to be the true love he wasn't and put her on the payroll at a good beginning salary. It was Hal who had given her the Coxx campaign, that which she mistook for both life and meaning.

Sheila drove him to the Yankee Maid Motel and let Hal Orinsek seduce her even though she'd said no. She didn't know why. She just did. And the sex was great.

And what Sheila thought was: So what?

Hal bought out all the LifeSavers at the Motel Coffee Shoppe cash register and handed them, twenty rolls or so, to her in a brown paper bag.

"Little prezzy," he said. "Now back to work."

"Back to work," Sheila answered, happily peeling open a package of Pep-O-Mints. She'd burned a few calories. Now she'd consume a few and work would consume her and the candidate Coxx would trounce poor Mr. Gilmore, and from her point of view, all would be well.

The Wickett

Now, Bob Wickett knew he had a life. He knocked off his job around three. His deliveries had been done for hours by then, but there was usually something that needed fixing around the dairy, and work was work. Bob talked about his boy all the time. The guys at the dairy all knew how Boggy was doing. They all knew about what had happened with his mom. They all knew the story of how young Robert Jr. had turned his name upside down and had changed it from Bobby to Boggy in the first week of first grade because he wrote his *b*s upside down. The way Bob told it, that was the smartest move any boy could make. Because of the boy, the boss knew Bob needed all the extra he could get and he was pretty good about it. Bob could have kept himself busy until six, but he'd told his Boggy to get on back from school early. Bob hadn't been around most of the week, and a kid needed a dad. Bob thought maybe they'd head out, get a few burgers. The kid could chow down three, four Big Macs and have room for two bags of fries and a shake. But what kid, what boy, Boggy's age couldn't?

So what has a dairy truck driver and his hungry son to do with Miss Sheila Jericault and her starving soul?

Everything.

Boggy lay on the grass out in front of the house, waiting for his dad and eating LifeSavers one at a time. He did not crunch them the way Sheila did. Having reached the age of twelve and a half, Boggy had come across a cruncher or two, but the way he saw it, crunchers missed the whole point of the hole in the middle, which was the whole point of a LifeSaver. The right way, the kid way, went like this: Avoid the green until there is no other choice. Always favor the red. Insert flat and let it make a colored stripe down your tongue. Get up off the grass or the couch or wherever you're lazing about and run to a mirror. Admire your colored stripe. Remove the LifeSaver from your mouth. Point your tongue and then stick its pointy tip through the widening hole. Pop the candy back in. Let the LifeSaver get as thin as it can. This takes time. And patience. Eventually, take it out to check your progress. Hold it up to the light and try to see through the color. Then the hole. Then put it back in your mouth, taking care not to bite until the hole is gone, which can only happen, if it is happening right, when the candy has dissolved into a tiny crescent. Then begin again with your next-favorite color.

Boggy dug his thumbnail into the wrapper and marked off the next in line, a yellow, when his dad pulled up.

"How was the test?" said Bob.

Boggy slid the yellow under his tongue for storage and wondered in passing if the first yellow after so many reds would be able to turn his tongue orange. "Aced it."

"No shit."

"I got a ninety-nine," said the boy. He knew his dad would be proud. Bob was always proud and right to be. Boggy was one of those kids a dad prays to get, and Bob, who didn't do much praying, didn't know what it was he'd done so right in the world to get so goddamned lucky. He heard guys saying stuff down at the dairy. Stuff about their sons. Drink. Smoke. Drugs. Trouble. But not Boggy. Bob had pulled through high school on account of fixing the principal's car for free. Boggy was straight A's all the way and not a snot about it either.

"Ninety-nine. What's that?" he teased. "You were taking the day off, or what?"

Boggy took the car keys out of Bob's sagging pocket. "Can I drive?"

"No," said his father. "We're going down 8A. Too many cops."

"I'll get out before 8A." Boggy jumped up and down. A big chunk of the time, Bob saw Boggy as a muddy-faced kid who couldn't get enough candy, and another chunk of the time, he saw him as the man he would grow to be. In the remaining chunks, what he saw—what part of Boggy he saw—changed minute by second. "Yes!" said the little boy. "Say yes! Pleeeeease!" And now, older. "C'mon. Dad. I'm as good as half those jackasses got a license. You know that."

Bob didn't want to say no. "Okay. But you pull over when I say, and not a word about it. Clear?"

Sheila Jericault probably saw Bob and Boggy. Bob and Boggy probably saw Sheila. Same as they all saw the other two hundred fifty people who happened to be at the Farbury Road McDonald's that day and that particular hour. It wasn't like they knew each other and ought to have said hello (though they, not to mention all the yellow- and pink- and white-skinned humans alive, were extremely long-lost cousins at a remove of about a hundred thousand years).

Anyway, Bob and Boggy lingered at their table. Watching the road, watching the girls who traveled in threes, too old yet for Boggy and way too young for Bob. Father and son compared the sauce on the Big Mac with the heft of the Quarter Pounder. Bob dipped a french fry in a puddle of ketchup and said, "The secret here, boy, is timing and heat, which may, for that matter, be the secret to everything in the goddamn universe, so remember it. You got to get the grease to just the right boil so it's going to sizzle up nice, and then you whack that wire basket in and sear the little bastards. Not cook the shit out of them. Just a good sear."

"I read it's sugar," said Boggy, dangling a fry at his lips. "Got nothing the least to do with timing. They put sugar on so they taste good. Simple."

"Bull," said his dad, though he'd read the same thing. "You're saying sugar on a potato? Or maybe these ain't potatoes? Maybe who knows? We got no reason to trust these guys. For all we know, these fries might be cardboard. Not even fresh cardboard. Recycled. How'd you like that? Little sugar. Little ketchup. Who could tell? You think, Boggy? Cardboard with sugar. Yum yum. No timing involved."

Sheila sat, not listening to any of this, though their voices carried and she might have heard it. She sat in a plastic chair anchored to the wall, but she wasn't particularly aware of that, either. She was reliving the triumph of that sun-kissed Coxx fund-raiser. She had already forgotten the sex with Hal. That was done. Over. At least until the next time. Coxx, however, was a going thing. He was a winner who had yet to win, officially win. And until he won, until he was Mr. Congressman and that last vote was cast on November third, her job was neither over nor done. She jumped up from her chair and swung her purse over her shoulder. What had she been thinking? she asked herself. She had no time to sit. So she vacuumed her Big Mac down her throat on the way out the door. She had no time to taste what it was that filled her hungry belly. No time to chew, much less notice the secret sauce that Boggy Wickett swore made all the difference. She'd drink her Coke in the car. She had to go.

The Next Day

The next day was different. Still sunny. Still crisp. The leaves on the maples and oaks and birches and so on shook with such vivid yellows, such shouting reds, that it seemed preposterous to think they were actually dying. Sheila crunched four Pep-O-Mints at once and cursed. Death. The thought kept scratching at her. It had been slipping in between the good news all damned day, and even she couldn't miss it. The fund-raiser had topped their goal by two thousand dollars. The public had fallen in love with Kip Coxx and Polly and Kippy and Chip and that little Buddha-faced baby. What more? thought Sheila, trying to rule the contents of her mind. Why the prickle? She stopped her car at a farm stand along Route 8A, bought a gallon of apple cider, a half peck of apples, and a twelve-pound pumpkin. As he transferred the apples from a flimsy wooden basket to a plastic shopping bag, the farmer started gabbing about Kip Coxx. He'd never voted against Gilman, had never even considered it, his daughters had gone to high school with one of the Gilman girls, but he was now behind Coxx one hundred percent. He asked Sheila if she wanted to buy a COXX FOR CHANGE bumper sticker. She gave him another buck and stuck the sticker to the cider jug. The farmer did not know who she was. She liked that. She liked the whole thing. So why death? she thought, and reached for the car phone, which whispered fragments of an argument between two men. And then went dead. For no reason she could name, Sheila suddenly feared for the health of the candidate. Rather than finish her errands, she turned the car around and drove the half hour back to headquarters, imagining emergencies, cursing the bending country roads.

Kip was fine. More than fine. "Great," said Sheila uncomfortably. "Fabulous. Great." She poured herself some cider and sat on the edge of a wobbly card table covered with videotapes from the last focus group. She popped one into the VCR. There was Hal, smiling Hal, charming Hal, conducting a spirited chat with a dozen folks glad to have their say. Sheila's eyes wandered from the set. She could not will her ears to hear words. It occured to Sheila that she might need a break. For a second, maybe less, Sheila let her eyes close, and in that frightening second she thought again about death—not dying exactly, but ceasing to be. She shot her empty paper cup across the room into the wastebasket. "Two points." She made herself pick up a sheaf of polls. New stuff on the major concerns of the undecideds. "So what are we going to do about hooking these babies? We can't spare a soul. We need them with us." Sheila was too busy for a break and she didn't like them anyway. Empty space to be filled. That's what a break was. Something to fix. "Gimme a doughnut," she ordered, knowing her wish would be fulfilled as it was spoken, because she was in charge. "I gotta eat."

Two hours after midnight, Sheila put her feet up on the office couch and, with a pile of papers on her chest, she slept. She hadn't wanted to go home to sleep in the comfy bed in the slightly shabby, slightly frilly little dormer apartment that she had rented for the length of the campaign. She hadn't wanted to go home, not at all. She was dizzy. And she was scared, as well she should have been, for this day was not the day before.

At exactly the same time Sheila fell asleep, Bob Wickett and his boy pulled on their thermals and wool and headed over to Jack March's farm to help out. Mrs. March had called.

There were two cows, Midge and Lucy, both bellowing at the peak of their labor. Midge had herself a breech birth, but it looked like the calf would survive. Jack was handling that. But Lucy howled and threw her eyes back like she was ready to succumb in agony if she didn't get a hand and fast. Her bloody-faced calf wailed and thrashed its head, but it could not get loose of its mother. Bob tied Lucy's hind legs so she wouldn't kick. Boggy reached his hands deep inside the poor cow and eased her hundred-and-ten-pound newborn into this world. Quick, Bob squeezed the colostrum out of Lucy's teat and Boggy pushed the calf's face to the steaming bucket. Bob hugged his boy. "You have the gift," he told him.

The breech was born just after, and once they all washed up, Jack March's wife made a celebration breakfast with bacon and eggs and pancakes and biscuits and cream coffee, hot. Boggy's mother had been gone since before Boggy knew how to crawl, and though Bob was the best father he knew how to be, he plain never cooked like that. "You stay," he told the boy as he buttoned his CPO. "I got to get to work." He threw the car keys to his eleven-year-old son. Hell with the law, he thought. The boy had been man enough that morning. "I'll get a lift over with Palcewski. You drive straight home, and I mean like an arrow. No wanderin'," he said. "And careful."

Bob cut across the Marches' orchard, thinking about the way that boy made him feel so proud his ribs could break from it. Busy with love, he had no eye for the camouflage-painted military-surplus truck that was coming up fast alongside, filled with boys whose clothes matched the truck, whose guts were loaded with twelve hours' worth of beer and whose guns were loaded and cocked. He was thinking of the way Boggy pulled out that calf and wondering if the boy would be a vet. Or a doctor, he thought, and he pictured that clearly in his mind. He had no eye for evil just then. But it was there anyway, ungodly and all too human, shameless, mindless, merrily murderous. The boys were having themselves a good time. They wanted to shoot and they shot at what moved, not caring what it was but just that they killed it.

Bob wasn't expecting a slam in the belly. He felt the heat and knew he had a bullet in him. His very first thought was, Why?

He didn't see who did it, though he thought he'd heard laughter. Laughter? It made no sense to him. He struggled to make sense prevail. He was walking in the orchard. Thinking of his boy. It was impossible. He couldn't be shot. Shot why? Bob fell back, momentarily cradled by the low branches of an apple tree before he hit the ground. When he opened his eyes, he saw wild geese all around him. He smelled the sweet air. The bright sky nearly blinded him. I'm fine, he thought, just a tumble. And then he felt the hot pain and a poisonous fury filling his veins as the blood ran out of his body. Who did this? What bastard? he thought. And, Why? What was the reason? He didn't have to see the blood. He saw the steam rise from the stinking blood-soaked wool. He was dying, dying right there on the wet grass alone for no reason.

If Jack March's wife hadn't prevailed upon her husband to quick run over and gather up just eight apples so Boggy could taste her blue-ribbon turnovers fresh from the oven, who knows how long it would have been until they found Bob Wickett under the branches?

The apples remained ungathered, the turnovers unmade. Wickett opened his eyes and saw the suffering face of his young son.

The Twig Snaps

When it comes to you—and by you, I do not necessarily mean you personally, but your species as a whole—it is often difficult to steer clear of despair. The power of nature never seems enough. Still, you have your moments of wisdom, often accidentally. For instance, in Bob Wickett's contemplation of fried potatoes, he inadvertently described the manner in which he was able to spurn death's stinging kiss. Timing was indeed everything, both in the matter of losing his life and again in the matter of having it returned to him. I neither did nor undid anything. And as for my will, I assure you I had none in this case, or none I chose to exercise.

It was only an hour or two later that morning when Sheila Jericault woke to the hiss of an automatic coffee maker. She switched on the radio and tidied the papers that had scattered on the floor. The announcer mentioned the mysterious shooting after the market report, but Sheila did not seem to hear the awful news. She was dwelling on the drop in unemployment, which was, for some reason beyond my capability for understanding, bad for the stock market. It was also bad for Kip, who didn't want things to get better before he could take credit for making them so. At the seven o'clock newsbreak, the shooting registered and Sheila said, "Oh, shit." Not because a man had been mysteriously shot in an orchard, but because it required that she prepare Kip's opinion on a subject related to guns. Dicey. She scribbled her thoughts on a Post-it just in case he was asked to comment: *Shooting this a.m. nr. Farbury. No details known. You abhor random violence, family violence, drug violence, careless hunting accidents, etc., etc., etc. Touches us all (pls. stress!). When elected VIGOROUSLY FIGHT AGAINST. You pray for him and his family and as a father yourself blah blah blah. NOTE: Deeply saddened if he croaks. (Funeral?) DO NOT MENTION GUN CONTROL.*

She put the Post-it in a place where only Kip would find it and thought once more briefly about how the gun issue could really fuck things up. She checked the clock and booted up the computer and reviewed the AP wire. She revised her to-do list and poured herself a cup of something that passed for coffee. She rechecked the clock and then, because Kip was due at a Concerned Commuter Coffee Klatsch in less than an hour, she rushed home to shower and change.

But the narrow twig upon which Sheila's life was resting had snapped. Perhaps in this matter I am less innocent. I do not care for confession, but I will say: Perhaps.

Sheila tried to be the self she knew, but she wasn't. She was frightened because she felt so frightened and sad, and she didn't know why. What should have been simple wasn't. She took off her tired clothes and ran a bath. She told herself a bath was what she needed, a nice, warm bath. And in the bath she cried a little. That was what she needed, a good cry. The phone rang. She stood and staggered. The ringing stopped. "A hot bath can make you dizzy," she said as if someone else in the room required an explanation. Sheila couldn't explain why she couldn't stop crying. Cry it out, she told herself, wondering what "it" was. She flopped on her bed and cried and cried and found that there was a mossy, rich luxuriousness to her despair. So thick, so rare, so wide and lush, so unexpected. It was more than a feeling. It was almost a place. And in it she wore a red cashmere shawl. Then the wayward thoughts, the uninvited fear, sharp and heavy, blocked her way out, closed her in. "I've got to go," she pleaded. She made herself stand and strap on her watch. That helped. She checked the time. "Jesus Christ. I got to get a wiggle on here."

She had ten minutes when she should have had twenty. Sheila was never late and usually early. Nonetheless, she drove the speed limit exactly, as if following all the rules would protect her from the sentence that had been spoken, just once, but clearly, in her head. This is the day I am going to die. That's what she heard. "Cut it out," she argued. "I don't have time for this shit." But whatever it was wasn't over. She started to sing. Loud. Louder than her thoughts. A song from her childhood. "Once there was a silly old ram . . ."

Kip shook hands with everyone who entered the railroad station. The volunteers stood at the door and the ticket window, offering all the commuters free coffee and Danish, good Danish with enough jam in it, not crap from the Stop & Shop. "Nice touch," said Sheila to a volunteer named Mary, a woman who always seemed to have endless time.

"You look pale," said Mary.

Sheila touched Mary's arm and said, "Did you ever have a time when you were scared for no reason?"

"Yeah, every twenty-eight days like clockwork. That's just the devil playin' wit' you." Mary handed her a raspberry twist. "You got hormones is all. Don't give in."

"I won't," pledged Sheila. She moved toward the center of the crowd to blend in and listen to what the voters said among themselves. Hal Orinsek winked at her. Her heart beat between her eyes. She turned to a pudgy man in a pale gray suit and tried to smile and was shocked to hear herself asking the question again, "Did you ever have a time when you were just scared?"

"Did I ever not?" he replied.

Stop it, she told herself. She told her mind to stop stop stop, and the man's face disappeared. He was gone. She was gone. And when she opened her eyes, there was a crowd around her. There was a cup at her lips. She sipped the water. Her first thought was of the candidate. "God, how embarrassing," she said. No one seemed to hear her. She tried to pull herself up. Someone held her down on the floor.

"Lie still," came the order. "You're bleeding."

She looked. There was blood everywhere, but knew she had not been wounded. Where was the blood coming from? Lower. Between her legs. How? She didn't understand. "Shit," said Sheila. Or maybe she just thought it. "I'm sorry." Her hands were tingling. She couldn't close them.

Two ambulance technicians slid her legs—she knew they were her legs, they were where her legs should be—into a pair of plastic trousers. "This is going to feel a little tight, but it'll keep the blood in," a man's voice said. Then the pants inflated. Sheila shut her eyes. She didn't want to see Kip. She didn't want to see any of this. She let herself be carried by strangers. Heard the siren, faintly, as if it were far down the highway, far from her.

"I ought to cut back on coffee," she offered. One technician poked her with a needle. The other held her open hand.

Sheila Jericault was dying. And she didn't know why. An orderly shoved her blood-soaked clothes in a black plastic garbage bag. More needles, more blood, yellow bags of plasma as they docked her in Intensive Care. She stared at the traveling lights on the heart monitor, watched the line that meant her life, as her hands and legs swelled to indecency and her blood pressure plunged. Her hematocrit was 22. No good. She knew that and not much else. Two nurses, both wearing tags that read ELLEN, worked in fervent silence. "Please talk to me," she begged. "I'm scared."

"I'm scared too," answered one of the Ellens, and Sheila was glad and grateful.

She was losing blood faster than the nurses could put it in. Bag after bag of other people's blood hung on a silvery rack, dripped into her useless arm as her heart pumped and pushed life's fluid out like excrement. The blood she had and made in her own body was gone. Whose blood ran in her veins now? Her body refused to keep it.

The Ellens together seemed to have more than four hands as they turned dials, read meters, pressed and tested, and yet still sponged her and stroked her and strived to keep her poor body clean. Cleanliness was all she had that felt anything near right, and she hadn't much of that. "What *is* this?" she asked.

"We don't know," answered the gentle nurse.

A doctor named Hallerman would walk by, linger, touch her arm. His eyes were bluer than hers, practically violet, and his lashes and brows were very black, but his hair and beard were striped with gray. Whatever he was doing, all he was doing, he was doing to save her life, and Sheila needed to see his very blue eyes. She couldn't sleep. The nurses wouldn't let her sleep. She looked for his beautiful eyes and asked herself this:

Was there anything, any one thing, any ten things, she could have done that day or at any other time in her life so that she would not now be dying? Knowing whatever she knew at the time, she could only answer no. No. She hated that answer.

And in her mind, her still-working mind, Sheila tried to insist to herself that she wanted to live. I want to live, she thought, but she did not know why. No reason, no *real* reason came to her. I want to live, she thought, trying to feel the want all the way, the will—to live, to live, to live—and failed. It felt truer to say, I don't want to die. But what Sheila felt most of all was that what she wanted didn't count. Her body had betrayed her.

She prayed: Our father Who art in heaven Hallowed be thy name Thy kingdom come Thy will be done On earth as it is in heaven. That was as far as she got. Thy will be done. She said it over and over. That was the truest thing she knew. And in her honesty, she asked a daring question. If she died . . . What? Who needed her past the point of campaign victory? Who needed *her*? Who did she love? She told herself the truth. The truth was, no one. Then she began to mourn. And it came to her: She had gradually, even gladly, hollowed out her soul. So she wouldn't hurt. So she wouldn't lose. So she wouldn't need. She hadn't missed it. Damn it. She'd liked it that way. That was the truth and the truth was all she could give herself. But now, in the nothing of her atrophied heart was more nothing. No reason why. Thy will be done, she prayed, and I was moved by the unexpected modesty of her request. She asked for nothing but that.

"Sweetheart, how can we get in touch with your parents?" an Ellen asked.

"My mother's on a cruise."

"What cruise?"

"Carnival." Sheila laughed. Ellen had the decency to laugh with her. "I want to know everything," said Sheila.

"You will. Try to have some faith in us."

"In you," Sheila answered.

"Yes."

Sheila tried to have faith in the Ellens and found it easier than trusting to great invisibilities like me and the others of my kind. She could see the Ellens. See what they were doing.

"We can't locate the source of the bleeding until we stabilize you," said Dr. Hallerman.

"Do whatever you want," she told his eyes. She commended

herself to him then. Shivering savagely, her lonely body fought without faith or resignation. To live. To live, her heart and brain grabbed at the scant oxygen, estranging themselves from her less vital extremities. There was not enough life force for all of her. She understood that. Hallerman made an incision in her chest. She didn't feel it. He tried to insert a catheter in her aorta so that when—he said if but meant when—she went into shock, they could pump blood straight into her heart. It didn't work. He couldn't get the catheter through. Too late. Her pressure was too low. No salvation there.

Nor did Sheila's struggling spirit feel any welcome from the dying side.

Ellen brought a permission form for an arteriography. Ellen fitted her hand over Sheila's hand and pressed her fingers around a pen. Ellen helped her lean forward to sign. Sheila signed and vomited. She felt she was nothing but the turf on which this internal revolution was being fought. Why was it against her, her body? What part was the traitor? And what part had warned her? Her weak hand was an ally. It would not release Ellen's hand. "Come," said Sheila. "Please." One Ellen came. And the tubes and the monitors and the blood all came too. The blood. Cleanliness had become almost impossible, but it mattered less as the hours—Were they hours? She could not tell—passed.

And Sheila understood this: If she was going to die, it didn't matter if she died in a puddle of bloody shit. If she died in a puddle of foulest black, it was because her body had given out and that was all. It seemed as dignified a death as any. Death was immune to decorum. Death was easy and it was easy to die. What was hard was giving up life. She wasn't done. No, she thought, she had not started. She had not lived. And all the goodness and the beauty, the compassion and the Grace? She had dismissed it. So what? she had said, and even so, this Ellen still held her hand, sharing the living warmth of her own body.

She did not let go. Sheila whispered, "Thank you," but she could not hear her own voice.

Ellen studied the heart monitor. Hallerman stood within a cloud of doctors as someone shaved Sheila's pubic hair. She could not see who held the razor. A catheter scraped its way upward, a little scope, a searcher. More needles. More blood. The radioactive dye made her body volcano-hot inside. Veins afire, she watched a television screen. She saw her guts being probed by a little hooked tube. And then Hallerman shouted, "Perfect! Perfect!"

After forever, she found his eyes again.

"She can't sign anything," he said. He put his soft hand on her cheek. "Sheila. Do you consent to an operation?"

"Yes."

"Were there any witnesses?" asked Hallerman.

None. Only he had heard her. Sheila willed herself enough strength to speak once more. "I consent," she said, giving in to her fate.

Now they began. A new woman came to her with a purposeful look on her face. She held a black mask in her hand, and Sheila knew why she was there. No. That was too much. She could not bear to yield her consciousness. No. Her body shook with an immense violence. Her teeth rattled and chattered as every part of her joined with her soul to chase away the coming darkness. No. She stared at the eggshell-colored ceiling. Holes in the tiles. Little holes in rows. Where was Hallerman? Where were his eyes? If this was to be her last certain moment of life, she wanted his eyes. The anesthetist brought the rubber mask toward her mouth and nose. Sheila turned her head. "It's all right," the anesthetist lied. "This is only oxygen." Sheila accepted the lie and the mask as her body still shivered and fought. And though she knew instantly she had been tricked, she could do nothing about it. She felt a needle, one more needle. Rows of holes.

And that could have been it. That could have been all there was to her life. The end.

But Sheila did not die and leave her newfound discomfort behind. Sheila survived, and for reasons entirely beyond her control. You can call that destiny if you wish. I will neither confirm nor deny. Whatever it was, Sheila found herself alive, and the excruciating truths that had blessed and cursed her dying moments were at least as alive as she was. And she was stuck with these unchosen companions.

How could I but delight at the promise of her predicament?

Life After Life

You might think that Sheila rejoiced beyond measure at the shock of finding herself alive, but you would be wrong. She had seen too much for that. She looked up at the holes in the ceiling and knew that her other life, the one she'd been a heartbeat short of losing, was over anyway. She could not reenter it. She could not pretend the hole she'd seen wasn't there, or get busy and forget about it.

Now what?

That was the question, and it was immense. She suspected that the reason why, the reason to live, was not on the list she'd already explored ignored deplored. She wondered if, in order to find it, she would have to come up with a whole new interior, a whole new self.

She had no answers and her natural impatience tortured her. She was desperate to know—know instantly—and be relieved of the desperate burden of wondering.

But she knew nothing, not even how to search.

As she lay in her hospital bed and for some time after, she did not feel that, perhaps, she had been touched by Grace. If, for a second now and then, a sensation resembling gratitude presented itself, it was quickly overwhelmed by nearly intolerable, itchy irritation. That constant, simple, unanswerable question had burrowed deep under her skin and built a home there.

Now what?

At first, in the first few days, Sheila was surrounded by flowers. Flowers from everyone who wanted a favor. Flowers from everyone she owed. No friends, no real friends. Why should she have flowers from friends? She'd shed everyone who wasn't useful. And that made her more than sad. Kip and Polly had sent two dozen yellow rosebuds on the verge of opening, along with a note wishing her a speedy recovery written in Polly's hand. She'd signed Kip's name as well as her own. What the note did not include was any offer to help. It was an unbidden reminder that Sheila was going to have to pay quite a bill for this life she now had. The Coxx campaign had not provided health insurance for its workers. Who knew what the cost would be? She couldn't bear the thought, so she shoved it aside and stared at the purple and yellow irises sent by Mary the volunteer. Of all the flowers, only these seemed beautiful.

Sheila tried not to jar herself as she leaned forward to touch the petals. She heard laughter in the hall and tensed, falling back to her pillow in pain. It was the laugh of a certain thick-fingered nurse who insisted she stand and take half a dozen steps to nowhere and back several times a day. She hated the nurse who demanded she walk in pain. She hated pain and loved her morphine, because though she knew she'd been cut open, the morphine made her agony an abstraction. But the morphine only worked on her body. It did not blunt her bafflement. That she endured at full force.

Now what? Now what? Now fucking what?

Dr. Hallerman came to her bedside at night and in the morning. She waited for him and his eyes so blue she could and would and wanted to live in them. If he looked away, she waited to catch his gaze again like a baby finding its mother, knowing the eyes that gave it life from all other eyes and finding comfort there. When she looked at Hallerman's eyes, she didn't say, Now what? She knew what. But then he'd go. One morning he came and smiled at her and then, without warning (he thought it better that way), he removed the staples from her mean red scar, a rusty wound the length of a hunting knife. She screamed in shock. Screaming hurt worse than what he was doing, so she closed her eyes and tried to let the morphine carry off her pain. When he had finished, he gently touched the scar itself. She felt the surprising softness of his fingertips and the tenderness of her bruised skin as one undivided sensation. She closed her eyes again. Then he told her he was taking her off morphine and prescribing Tylenol 3 for pain. "And the good news is," he said, "I'm sending you home."

She cried. He asked her if the pain was too much. "No," she lied.

"Good," he said. He was happy with her answer. "You were an interesting case."

"Is that a compliment?" Sheila asked.

"Compliment?" Hallerman contemplated Sheila's joke as if it had been a serious question.

"I still don't understand exactly what happened. To me, I mean. To my body."

Hallerman sighed, and then smiled. "Well, under the circumstances, I can't blame you for being distracted. From the top: What you had is called an AVM, arteriovenous malformation. Extremely unusual for someone your age. Extremely." He drew her a diagram of her heart, her arteries, her veins, with arrows that pointed which way the blood was supposed to flow. Then, with a scribble of ink, he showed her how one of her arterioles had suddenly burst and messed up the circuit, spitting out her blood in heartbeat spurts. It was a defect in the way she was made, a tiny congenital time bomb ticking since before she was born. "Clear now?"

Sheila nodded.

"It could happen again," he said. "Or not. No way to know."

"Are there odds? I mean . . ."

Hallerman shrugged. He knew what she meant. "No way to know. Just live your life. Don't wait for the sword to drop."

Within the hour, Sheila's mother arrived at the hospital, happy and tanned from her Carnival cruise. She was thrilled, just thrilled at Sheila's helplessness and didn't bother to disguise it. She hadn't particularly liked her daughter once she developed a mind of her own, but she had loved having a baby. Abloom with nostalgia, she wanted to whisk Sheila off to New Jersey, to her condo at the Wildwood Retirement Community. She wanted to hang lacy curtains and paint the guest room pink, which had been Sheila's favorite color when she was five. But Sheila wasn't willing. She wanted to go home. Home to her rented dormer apartment on Currier Street. Home to a place that she'd barely noticed before. A place where she'd slept. Sometimes. Sheila's mother argued but gave in. She had Jerry, her tanned beau, carry Sheila up the two flights to her bed and sent him away. "Mommy will take such good care of you," she chirped as she punched two throw pillows and wedged them under Sheila's head. Sheila stared at the unsettled dust as it recovered from her mother's blow, dancing sideways and down.

Though Sheila craved silence in which to make sense of what happened to her, what had happened did not actually make sense. And, furthermore, even if she had the desire, she had not the physical strength to stand and shuffle to the phone, order a pizza with Coke, rake up some cash, walk to the door, and pay the delivery boy, much less carry the slight weight of a pizza box to her little dining room table. Her weakness made her a prisoner. She could not take care of herself. So her mother shopped and cooked and tidied up and stoically slept on the couch. Since Babs, short for Barbara, which was Sheila's mother's name, was in paradise, fat with half-imagined memories of Sheila's perfect infancy, she was less inclined to pick and pry at the imperfect woman her daughter had become. Sheila ate the milky rice pudding her mother insisted had always been her favorite and was glad that Mommy was there to help her. To a point.

After that point, Sheila took secret leave of her mother. She wasn't missed. Babs neither required nor wished for a second voice to add the unbidden and unpredictable, as second voices tend to do.

Sheila stared out her third-floor window, stealing a sliver of silence from the present chat chat chat chat chat so constant that it was a form of quiet in itself. She stared out the window and tried to predict the moment, the minute and hour, certain exquisite burgundy maple leaves would be let loose from their branch. It was a silly game and she never won, but she played. The leaves were her companions. They fell from the tree, each one teasing gravity, nearly promising never to touch the ground. As if there were no rush to winter, they fell, each one in its own slow moment, from that tree and the other trees on Currier Street. One, a red-tipped golden leaf, had deep green veins that looked like a tiny tree had branched within the leaf. Sheila watched it closely, idly wondering if the tiny tree had tinier leaves that were falling within the leaf itself as it danced and floated, whirled and dipped for so long, minutes and minutes, that Sheila wondered if she was seeing the impossible become possible. What if, she thought, there was one leaf, one single leaf in a the world, that was not required to follow the laws of gravity? What if, because Sheila was still, because she was watching, she had seen what no one before had ever seen and might never see again?

The wind rose and the leaf rose with it. Then balls of ice, a hailstorm, stripped the branches at once, like an angry hand slapping the leaves to the ground, where they lay wet and shiny, glued to the mud.

Sheila went to sleep that night mourning the leaves and the end of the game. Now what?

When she woke, as her mother complained of the cold wind slicing through the gap between the window sash and sill, Sheila saw what the leaves had hidden, what they and the now-barren hedges and the flowers and so on had been planted to hide long ago. Lives. The lives of the people on Currier Street.

Currier Street was a place where the wealthy lived if they preferred to live in town. Behind the white houses with rows and rows of sparkling windows, lives were hidden. The residents of Currier Street had the means to afford their privacy. Only winter exposed them, and then curtains might be drawn. Or the houses might be abandoned while the residents traveled to warmer places where, again, their privacy would remain intact.

If Mr. and Mrs. Robert V. Onthwaite, major contributors to the Coxx Election Fund, had not gone to the island of St. Martin, Sheila would not have been living among the wealthy on Currier Street noticing the extent of the privacy these homes offered, she would have been down at the dreary Yankee Maid sleeping badly and hearing noises through the walls. She considered herself lucky that the Onthwaites wanted to ward off burglars. Though they'd locked and alarmed the house so that no one, including Sheila, could enter their living quarters without alerting the police, the Onthwaites wanted what they called a presence. Sheila was chosen to be that presence. They had rented her the little dormer with its tiny bath and alcove kitchen. The flat had its own back entrance, and the price they charged made it possible for them to deduct a portion of their utility costs as a campaign donation.

So. Sheila the presence stared out her window. She stared past the stripped branches and into the windows of the stately house across the street. And though she did not know it at the time, she was staring at her fate.

The Foreign Element

Within the stately house that contained the fate for which Sheila had to wait lived a family. Sheila began to see a pattern. After the family—a woman, three children, a man—left, the husband for work, the children for school, the woman, wherever, the house across the street seemed at rest for a while and then there was a dark brown face. It appeared in one window, lingered for an instant, perhaps watching a cardinal on the lawn, and disappeared. Then it stopped cautiously at the next window, and the next. Not as if it were looking for something or someone, but as if the simple act of looking was a devilish risk. Stealing a glance. Literally stealing a glance. It, she, saw Sheila sitting at her window watching and ducked behind a sheer curtain as if she were so small and slight the transparent cloth would hide her. "Something is off over there," Sheila remarked to her mother.

"Like what?"

Sheila told her.

Babs paused at the window. Saw nothing. Blotted her lipstick on a tissue. "You're projecting," she diagnosed. "As usual." Nonetheless, she was intrigued enough to glance at the name on the mailbox on her way out to the Grand Union. "The name is Babahani," she said when she returned.

"Arab," said Sheila.

"Baa baa black sheep . . ." sang her mother as she unpacked the groceries.

"Rich Arab."

"Sweetheart," Babs sighed as she filled a glass bowl to the rim with clementines. "Is there any other kind?"

"What are they doing here?" Sheila asked.

Sheila's mother set a kettle on the stove and sighed once more at her daughter's question. "It's a free country." She opened a package of Fig Newtons and arranged them on a flowered plate. "Don't you need to go potty?"

"I went," said Sheila. "As long as I move slowly, I seem to be okay."

"That's wonderful," said her mother sadly. If Sheila could walk, however much the pain, it meant she would soon be able to manage for herself and Babs would no longer feel so splendidly, utterly essential.

The kettle shrieked. Sheila returned to her view. There was no more to see. The phone rang. It was Kip Coxx. "Kip!"

"Sheila, you have no idea how we miss you," he blurted, a seductive urgency saturating his voice. "No idea."

"I think I do. I keep thinking there's a call I ought to be making or a tape to look at, y'know. This peace and quiet . . . I miss you guys."

"You want to come in and work?"

"I can't. I can barely lift a coffee cup."

"Oh." This was not the answer Kip wanted, and as you recall, Kip was a man defined by what he wanted.

"You sound funny."

"Old eagle ears, that's you."

"Problem?"

"Crisis. Total crisis. Fact is"—Kip cleared his throat and continued hoarsely—"I need you."

Sheila forgot the brown face. She forgot herself. She forgot mortality and the holes and the questions and rejoiced at the familiar thrill of a campaign crisis. "What's up?" she demanded, ready to take charge and work her old magic.

"Well . . ." said Kip. "I kind of . . . My wife . . ."

"If you don't tell me, I can't help."

"Polly has endorsed the incumbent."

"What?" Sheila shouted so loud it hurt her scar. "Get out of here. That's not funny."

"I'm not kidding."

Sheila waited silently, listening to the candidate's irregular breath until he was ready to speak.

"You see. I, uh, well, there's this woman who shall remain nameless . . ."

"Sue Tuthill?"

"Yes. And, uh, anyway. My wife. Well. Apparently, I, uh, left, uh, must have inadvertently forgotten, I don't know how the hell . . . a certain set of undergarments, uh, a particular pair of, uh, panties, uh, in the trousers of my dark blue suit. And Polly took it, I mean the suit, over to the Qwik Kleen . . ."

"She took your suit to the cleaners?"

"I didn't ask her to, goddamn it!"

"But she did. And?"

"And, um, the, uh, well, some change fell out on the counter, so she starts, right in front of the clerk, she's rooting around in my pockets . . ."

"And she found the panties."

"And started to scream. She's yelling, 'That son of a bitch,' and the . . ."

"When?"

"This morning. I just found out."

"And the clerk—apparently there were customers. . . . The

clerk, who's a fucking cousin of Ed Gilman, picks up the phone and . . . First the *Farbury Journal Express* . . . And they send over a goddamn . . ."

"Jesus H. Christ."

"And then Polly went on the air."

"She went on the *air?*"

"Turn on your fucking TV."

Sheila gestured to her mother. Polly Coxx was holding up a pair of cheap satin panties, torn here and there at the legs. Still dressed in her pink jersey jogging clothes, Polly Coxx aimed her bloodshot eyes past the reporter and straight out at the voting public. "Don't vote for Coxx," she said, and wept a moment. "He'll cheat you just like he cheated me."

"Wow," said Sheila, but she wasn't entirely shocked. Even she had had a quick, stupid screw on the office couch with the randy Mr. Coxx and wondered, within minutes of succumbing to her worst instincts, why Polly was so devoted to such a shit. Perfect Polly Coxx, faithful, apple-pie-baking Polly Coxx. "Jeez, that took balls," said Sheila, unable to hide her involuntary admiration.

"You're supposed to be on my side!" Kip whined. "What do I do? I could . . . I don't know . . . Maybe say she put them there herself? Maybe say she had a nervous breakdown?"

"Did she?"

"What difference does that make? We'll have to discredit her. . . . I mean . . ."

"Kip . . ." Sheila thought for a while and came to a conclusion that startled her but not me. "Polly is your wife and the mother of your boys." She didn't have the strength for this kind of crap. She didn't want anything to do with it. Not this. Not now, when she'd just been given her life for a second time. "Kip? You . . . We . . . I . . . We *all* invested a lot. We were *this* close to winning," she said, pinching the air in front of her. "And Kip?" Kip waited. "You totally fucked it up. Unfuckingbelievably. So you could ball Sue Tuthill. Man. I hope the earth moved, Kip. I really do. And by the way, please thank Mary for the flowers." Sheila hung up the phone. She couldn't bring herself to cry. She knew Polly's panty wave would make the national news at six and eleven. It was brilliant. "Ma," she said. "The campaign is fucked. I worked my ass off for that man. This was my own little masterpiece. Now what? No more Kip. No more campaign. And now I'm totally ground-zero out of the game and off-the-planet fucked," said Sheila. She wheezed with laughter. She didn't care if it hurt. It was supposed to hurt. She laughed and gasped and couldn't stop.

"And that's funny?" Babs shrugged, smiled, and handed her daughter a tangerine. "You think maybe the woman over-reacted? Maybe—I mean, the man's running for public office—and maybe she should have . . ."

Sheila laughed some more. When she could breathe, she said, "Mama, what would you do if you found out Jerry played around after all you've done?"

"Cut his balls off with a rusty knife," said her mother without any hesitation. "And stuff 'em in his mouth." Babs tittered, delighted by her daring dip into vulgarity.

Sheila peeled her tangerine. She was lost, she knew it. She was lost and fucked and free free free. Free and lost. She looked out the window, searching for the brown face. Where was that face? Not in the windows. Where was she? Was *she* lost? Then Sheila saw a tiny black-haired woman crouched on the lawn, surrounded by finches and juncos and squirrels. There she was. And she was feeding the animals bread from a pocket in her skirt. The squirrels took from her hand. She stroked their heads.

Sheila saw a red Miata turn onto Currier Street. Mrs. Ba-bahani's car. She recognized it. The tiny woman recognized it, too, recognized the sound of the motor or the tires on the road. The birds and squirrels scattered as she flew into the house and slammed the door before the car had even reached the drive-way.

43

Listing

B eing lost, Sheila decided to do what she had always done before she had known she was lost, before this dying business had come and dropped a load of questions on her tidy life. This was not an unwise choice, nor was it especially wise. The world is perpetuated by habit, cells meeting cells and doing the done thing, et cetera. Even gods do the same-old same-old. And as you have rather cleverly discovered, that which is seemingly the description of disorder, chaos, has a pattern of its own kind, though it may not be readily detectable. And so Sheila, in the tradition of the universe, decided to make one of her cherished lists. On the list she would write all the things she had to do. Then she would do them and tick them off, an activity that had, for her, an almost magical satisfaction to it. With great effort, Sheila got to her feet and walked to her desk. She took a pen and legal pad and returned to her spot at the window. What to do? she thought. And then, Do about what? Things, she thought. But she had so few things to do or do about that, at first, she could not write. In order to make it clear that she bloody well intended to take charge, she announced her plans to her mother. "I am going to make a list."

Babs didn't answer. She was thinking her own thoughts and she wasn't awfully happy. It was time to go. Sheila's mother sighed and inspected her yellowish arms. It was time to burnish that tan, time to turn brown and wear white creased trousers and dance the cha-cha-cha with Jerry, who called every night complaining of loneliness and restaurant food, who begged her to come home and whom she adored for that.

Sheila stared through the window to the windows across the street as if she might find a clue. She chewed her pencil as she watched her mother call her beau to make arrangements. Not looking at the page, Sheila began to write.

Nov. 1

To Do

What to Do

What the Hell to Do

Think!

She looked down and saw what she'd written. That wasn't a list. There were two ways to look at it, and Sheila tried both: She had so much to do and none of it nameable, and the tasks before her were so vast they defied list making; or, she had nothing pressing to be done, nothing that needed her urgent attention and thus had no list to make. Then she thought of something.

1. Call Hallerman re: appt.

Who else should she call? She had no friends who might visit. She hadn't had time for friends outside her work. Her ex-work. And her business friends wouldn't be calling her at home. Not now that Kip was a loser and she was history and there were no more favors to trade. She'd played by the same rules herself and did not need reminding. Hal wouldn't call. She knew that. She thought about calling Polly Coxx, of all people, but what would she say? I think you're amazingly brave and daring and you singlehandedly ruined my so-called career in a swoop, but not to worry your pretty head because I guess I don't care, and by the way, I slept with your shit of a husband, too? Not likely. She had no one. No one except Hallerman, her surgeon and savior. As Sheila saw it, she owed him her life. Maybe he'd want it.

2. Dive into H's Blue Eyes and Never Return
3. Fall Madly, Instantly in Love
4. Get Married in Two Weeks
5. Devote Rest of Life to Him and His Total Happiness

"Cute," said Sheila.
"What's cute?" said Babs.
"Nothing." Sheila called herself an idiot and started again. She asked herself what she honestly needed to do to make her second shot at life count for more than her first and tried again.

1. Be a Better Person
2. Do Good in the World
3. Be Happy

Sheila was disgusted. What kind of a list was this? If, just say if, she was sincere, and she wasn't even slightly sure she was sincere because she wasn't sure what sincere was, but if she *was* to go tick off this list, then how? If she was going to change for the better, then what? Where was the recipe? She hadn't seen it yet. Did it involve sensible shoes and some kind of dreadful good attitude? Maybe she'd lose everything she thought of as herself. Become a stranger. And what if she hated that stranger worse than she hated the one she was now? What if she didn't have it in her to be any better than what she'd become anyway, damn it? How the hell was she supposed to have any clue about good-doing if she didn't know what the hell good was? Christ. And as for happy? She wondered if it would be too late to take up smoking again. Smokers were happy smoking, as long as they put aside the idea it would kill them. And if they quit, they could be happy about that.

"Sheila, honey?" her mother interrupted. "How would it be . . . Do you think you could manage if, say, Jerry came to pick me up tonight?"

"Tonight?" Sheila glanced at her list. A bunch of dumb words. "You mean tonight?" What Sheila had faced at the moment she faced death could not be described as horror. Something like terror, yes. But not horror. What she felt now was horror. She was going to be alone. Alone, by herself, in herself, for herself. Life would have to start. Every day she would have to do everyday things: have breakfast, get dressed, go out, do this, do that. By herself. Pain or not. And what if she got absorbed in the everyday? *As if nothing had happened.* Same as before. In horror, Sheila realized what alone meant. ALONE. The wide world didn't give a damn if she made good on her new intentions. Either she would or she wouldn't, and only she would know. "Do you have to? Couldn't you, um, stay a week, maybe, till I'm stronger?" Sheila wondered if she would ever be strong enough.

"There's a ninety-nine-dollar superfare to Fort Lauderdale if you act now, as they say."

"If who acts?"

"Well, Jerry knows somebody. But I'll have to act, of course. I always do, Lord love him. He's utterly hopeless and helpless without me, you know."

Sheila sighed. Babs had made up her mind. "I guess I could manage," said Sheila. Whatever that was. And do good. Whatever that was. And be better. Whatever that was. Shit. "You've been wonderful. Really."

Sheila's mother discharged her daughter with a kiss and put on her coat. "I'll do a big shopping before I go and make you a batch of rice pudding."

"That would be good," said Sheila. "Thanks." She heard her mother start the car. It coughed and stalled, and Sheila waited, hoping for a change of plans, but Babs started it again. This time, no problem. "Terrific," Sheila moaned. "Now what?"

The Appointment

At the time Sheila made her postoperative appointment, she'd written it down neatly in small letters in
her leather-bound datebook. She need not have written in such tiny script. There was certainly plenty of room. The
datebook was jammed line by line into the margins up to two
days after she'd collapsed, and then nothing. Pure blank space.
As if perhaps the space would somehow fill itself in by itself,
Sheila checked and rechecked the datebook, lifting the red ribbon that marked the page on which she had written, examining
the pages before and after, then settling the ribbon down again
to rest. The appointment stood alone and continued to do so:

11 a.m. Dr. Hallerman
167 Applewood Road
Eat First

When the day came, she dressed all morning. The wound
made it difficult to move. Dressing was slow any day. But on
this day, she was going to see Dr. Hallerman's violet eyes, and

on the chance, the dreamish hope, that falling in love with her beloved lifesaver would handily give her all the purpose and meaning her wondering heart was looking for, she tried to look as nice as her condition would allow. None of her clothes really fit anymore. Even her makeup no longer matched her skin. She had not yet regained the color of vitality. Because she'd come too near to death to escape its drained and depleted tones, her face was blotchy and white. Still, she did her best, made adjustments, lining her blue eyes with black mascara, adding powdered pink to her cheeks, crumpling her red-gold hair to enhance its waviness.

Just before she set out, she rechecked her face in the rearview mirror, blotted away her pink lipstick, repainted her lips a deep pomegranate, and checked the map. It was an effort to walk to the car, much less drive it. She hadn't the energy for wrong turns. Applewood Road was out a ways past Route 8A, down 32. Sheila was disappointed. It was an odd location, she thought, and one that indicated that the doctor's office must be in his home. As Sheila figured it, a doctor's office in a doctor's home probably meant the doctor in question had a wife. But you never know, she told herself, aware that since her undeath that old saw was altogether too true for comfort. She carried one of Mrs. Onthwaite's floral throw pillows down the stairs. She told herself it was for her back, but she set it on the passenger seat.

The road was empty, and she drove too fast along 32. As she drove, she began enjoying the speed, feeling free by proxy, loving the wheels that carried her so much that she nearly missed the tiny white sign she was looking for. Applewood Road. Just after the turn, she passed a leafless orchard filled with wild geese resting on their journey to elsewhere. Across the way, she saw a tractor gnawing through a muddy barnyard toward a fenced-off field where cows stood shoulder to shoulder borrowing warmth from one another's bodies. A man ran at them, a farmer, she guessed, slapped one and then another and shouted, "Get!"

The road was bumpy. Each bump jarred her scar and the wound underneath, a torture that turned her romantic fantasies to rage. How could any thinking surgeon have his office on a road like this? What a bastard, she thought, forgetting her plans to love him forever.

"Damn him!" she ordered with such force you might have thought she had legions to do just that at her disposal.

Sheila moved along at seven miles per hour, pressing the brake each time she came in sight of a bump, easing the car up and over as gently as possible. She stuffed the throw pillow between her stomach and the steering wheel. "Damn that man," she chanted.

The road was long and, past the farm, it was mostly empty except for apple trees. Doubting herself, she stopped the car in the road and rechecked the address. 167 Applewood Road. Maybe she'd taken a back route. Maybe the road would change. It did not change, but a mile and a half down, she saw a farmhouse next to a concrete garage. Over the padlocked garage was a box-lettered sign. BOB'S AUTO BODY, it said. "Well, old Bobby-boy, you must be a genius," Sheila muttered. "This road would wreck a Jeep." There were no cars in the yard, just an ancient gas pump and a rusting pay phone. Sheila decided to call Hallerman's office. She pulled in and rested her head on the steering wheel until she had the strength to open the door. She walked carefully to the pay phone. Her quarter jammed. No surprise, thought Sheila. She'd expected that. Why shouldn't she expect that on a road like this? She was about to cry when she saw a man inside the garage, watching.

It was Bob Wickett. Bob put down his pen and reached for the silver gun on the lamp table beside his armchair. Picked it up. Set it down. Pressed his hands on the arms of the chair as he pushed himself to his feet. Then he slid the gun into his back pocket and walked slowly, dragging his shoulder along the wall as he made his way to the office door. There was a buzzer beside the door. He stood and waited for the woman to come closer. She did. She was just a woman, Bob thought, and she looked okay, but you could never tell. The way he saw it, everyone was suspect. Anyone could have pulled the trigger. He'd come up with a motto and he said it often: A gun doesn't care who shoots it.

"Hi," said Sheila.

He could see that she was weak by the way she moved. If he had to, he could overpower her. Or shoot. He pressed the buzzer and the door unlocked with a click. He pulled at the door until it gave and leaned his back against it to keep it open. He crossed his arms over his belly. He was panting. "In or out," he snapped. "I can't stand here forever."

Because Sheila had never met Bob Wickett, she could not have known how much he had changed since the shooting. His boy, Boggy, could have told her. First there was his dad who used to be great and let him do stuff. Then there was this other dad who got shot and died and then got a miracle that made him a grump. The old dad, the happy dad, he was gone. This dad didn't plan to be happy until whoever shot him got caught and got rightfully punished. This dad was scared because bad things could happen at any time, anytime at all, and not even an apple orchard was safe in this awful world. Boggy could have told her how this new dad didn't want him to do anything these days and how he didn't laugh, but Boggy was at school, where he wanted to be even more than before, so he could forget about the whole rotten thing and more or less be his regular self.

Bob Wickett couldn't get down to the dairy anymore. The boss told him he had a place when he was able, but Bob noticed he hadn't wasted any time getting another guy to take his truck. Bob brooded about that and a lot else. With nothing to do and time to do nothing but think, he thought. He sat around feeling the hole where the bullet went in every second of the day. He ran his finger over the scar, up and down, up and down, not even knowing, sometimes, that he was doing it. All day, he mulled over the details. How he left the Marches, gave Boggy the car keys, cut across. The facts. But the facts he knew stopped at just the point he needed them to start. Who raised up that gun? Who shot him? And why, damn it? In a moment, that someone, for no known reason, whoever, whoever it was, almost made his only beloved boy an orphan. Tried to rob Bob of what he had worked his life for: the joy, the pleasure, of seeing his own fine boy become a good man. Why? He wanted a reason, a good one. What happened to him was just too out of the blue for believing. Except that it had happened, and Bob was stuck with the truth of it. And that wasn't enough. Sometimes he almost blamed himself. If he'd finished breakfast with the Marches and his boy . . . If he'd have slept in late instead of giving Jack a hand . . . Sometimes he thought differently. Was that bullet for him? Or could it have been anyone that got shot? Could it maybe have been no one, never happened? He asked himself these things. He asked himself why, in a world full of people, he was that man. Why Bob Wickett? He thought about timing. Who could have been there in that exact spot that very moment with a loaded weapon and a mind to shoot it? Just about anyone. Could have done it for fun. Or hate. Or the heck of it. Did it matter for what? It might.

Bob Wickett was in no mood to be glad of surviving. He was in no mood to embrace his life. Bob wasn't done with the crime. He knew one thing more than he knew anything else: That person shouldn't just be free to keep on living life and going to McDonald's and making love or going fishing like he didn't pump a bullet in the gut of a man who'd done nothing to him. That was not justice. Bob Wickett couldn't live with that. He wanted to look the lousy scumball in the eye. Make him see

55

who it was he'd shot and make him pay. Sure, he was alive. But that was just a fucking miracle. The patched-up will of a sloppy god who shouldn't have let this happen in the first place, that's what Bob thought.

Bob had given up counting on the police pretty fast. They were as bad as everyone else. The way Bob saw it, they were so lazy they were practically conspirators. What did it get him that he'd donated every single year they came around collecting for that Benevolent Fund? Benevolent, ha! They weren't going to work themselves into too much of a sweat over him. No witnesses came forward. No one called the 800 number. Not no one. Just jokers who thought it was funny, that's all. Added up to nothing. So the cops took the number out of service. They got paid whether they found his shooter or not. When it happened, that clown Kip Coxx had personally said on TV that he'd fight and he'd get to the bottom of this, but he lost, damn fool. Now his wife was hogging Oprah and Phil with her personal problems and getting lots of sympathy. But who cared about him? Cops, like anyone else, would rather run with a winner, rather drive along the roads, clock speeders, drink coffee, eat lunch, and flirt at the counter. They told Bob there wasn't much in the way of clues. Nothing special about the gun that got him. And what they didn't say but he knew they meant was that there was nothing special about him, either, far as anyone but his boy was concerned.

At the moment Sheila drove up, Bob had been filling out forms. He was putting in for disability. The college money he'd been saving up since Boggy was two, so his boy would never be denied, so his boy could go to any school he could get into, so money would never block Boggy's road to the future, that was spent on doctors and hospital bills. That money was gone. For what? Not even the constant noise from the TV could stop him from thinking the stuff he thought, from passing his days and his nights just straining, pushing the edges of his memory until his head ached worse than usual, looking in his mind, looking for something his eyes had maybe seen at the time and not known they'd seen. The color of a car, a truck, a jacket, a face. He was looking and he believed it would come to him, if it was there to come. He was sure that if he ever saw the face of the one who shot him, he would have no doubts, he would just know. Screw the details. The truth would be revealed. Then he'd take his justice. Sometimes he called it that in his mind. And sometimes he called it something pure and clean as a beam of light: Revenge.

"Hi," said Sheila. "I wonder if you could please help me." She sensed something raw in this man and she was drawn to him. But she couldn't say why.

"What can I do you for?" said Bob. He reflected her smile with one of his own. Then he looked at her. "You okay?"

"Not really," she answered, grateful for the question. "Can I sit down?" He helped her. "I was looking for 167 Applewood Road."

"Well, Lord knows why, but you found it. You want a glass of water or something?"

"Please." Sheila had been so busy dressing to win the heart of her doctor, she'd forgotten she was supposed to eat.

"You want a candy bar?"

"Please."

Bob had a half-eaten Baby Ruth. He ripped the half in half, gave the unbitten part to Sheila, and popped the rest in his mouth. He waited until he was done chewing to take the gun out of his back pocket and set it on a gray metal cabinet in the corner of the room. "Got shot a few weeks ago. Almost died of it." He lifted up his sweatshirt. Showed off the bright scar that stained his gut. It was identical to Sheila's, as identical as two different scars on two very different bodies could possibly be. "Just luck that I didn't. So I got myself a gun. Never liked 'em. Now I got one and I mean to use it."

"That's how it goes," said Sheila quietly. She was overwhelmed by what seemed too much of a coincidence to be a coincidence. She wasn't sure how much more she wanted to say.

Bob straddled a folding chair, resting the ache. "So, what can I do you for?"

She mentioned the appointment, nothing more. Not yet. He dialed Hallerman's number and when a voice answered, handed her the phone.

"No no no. *Maple*wood, dear," said the nurse. "Maplewood. We were worried about you. Maplewood right behind the hospital, across from Lundy's."

"I don't know how . . ." Sheila stopped. She did know. "I don't understand," she said. This was true. The nurse fit her in at three. Sheila handed the phone back to Bob, catching his eyes with her own. Compelling, fearsome, his dark gray eyes were like thick electrical clouds on the verge of release. Sheila looked away. "My name is Sheila Jericault," she said. "I have something you gotta see." Carefully, modestly, she lifted her sweater.

Bob stared at the sewn-up gash that divided Sheila in half in undisguised awe. "Fucking epidemic," he muttered.

It Was Simple for Bob

T he odds against meeting the way they had met and
having twin scars like they had, and then knowing it,
had to be more or less equivalent to the odds against
catching a meteorite in a baseball mitt as it fell from the sky.
But it had happened, as these things do, and neither Bob nor
Sheila was inclined to waste a lot of energy rationalizing about
an unarguable oddity. To call it a mere coincidence seemed
disrespectful. It was more, they both agreed on that, but what?
And why?

Bob saw it as a sign that he had not been entirely forgotten,
that the Good Lord, the one he prayed to and raged at, had
finally decided to show a little courtesy, for chrissake. Not that
he was complaining (which he was), but he'd had a snootful.
On top of everything else, in the weeks since the shooting Bob
had had to listen over and over to folks going on about how
lucky he was. How thrilled he must be. How many times did
he have to hear how calm and unafraid he was supposed to be
now that he'd seen death up so close? And even though he'd
officially died and he understood why people would be curious,

when they asked about it, it wasn't like they really wanted to *know*. They wanted to hear what they wanted to hear: about the white tunnel of light, the dead relatives gladder to see him than they'd ever been in life, the beautiful angel music, like it was the ultimate good time. If he told the truth about how dying was for him, blacker and darker and bigger than anything he'd ever known, folks got upset. They got all disappointed. And he felt like he couldn't even die right, for chrissake. So he stopped telling the truth and started lying about something way too important to lie about. Threw in a few angels and light for the sake of the audience. Until Sheila came along. Thank God, he thought. Her, he told the truth. She listened without disappointment. She understood how he felt even though it wasn't pretty. And he was so relieved, he listened right back. Understood her looking up and wondering if rows of holes were the last thing she was ever going to see. A long time, ever. He understood helplessly not not not wanting to go. How he understood!

His eyes felt hot and teary when Sheila said good-bye. "Look," he said. He wrote his phone number on a lined receipt. "Maybe . . ." He put his hand on her shoulder and took it half-way back again so it fluttered indecisively between them.

"Don't worry," said Sheila. "At least you've got Boggy. He sounds like a good kid."

"Yeah. He's the whole ballgame."

"I'd like to meet him sometime."

"Yeah. Soon." Bob looked down at his feet lifting up and setting down one at a time in their own little dance. He made them stop. "Give me a couple weeks, get my strength, and if you need anything done, don't go paying some garage without you give me a call first."

"Don't worry." Sheila accidentally blackened a fingertip as she touched the sleeve of his greasy flannel shirt.

"You want me to take care of your oil before you go?" He

wanted to do something for her. He felt bad she was all alone. No man. No kid. "Free, of course." His skin was fuzzy gray and waxy, like a candle pulled from a dusty drawer.

"I'm fine. Next time. You'd better rest."

"Okay," he said. She was right. He was ready to fold. He'd let her have the best chair the whole time.

Bob had drawn her a map so she couldn't get lost twice. Applewood to Maplewood. Sheila set it on her dashboard and didn't refer to it. She knew she'd get there.

As I said, Sheila, like Bob, was convinced her detour was no accident. That fact was simple for Bob. But the same conviction made Sheila uncomfortable. She had no particular god to feel owed by and was generally not disposed toward embracing unexplained phenomena. Still, alone in the car she began to wonder. Sheila wasn't accustomed to asking *why me,* at least not in the extravagant, indulgent way Bob Wickett took for granted. But if she wasn't going to ask *why me,* and if it was no accident she'd come upon Bob Wickett, then some other *why* had to be asked. She considered Bob Wickett and his shiny new gun. She was frightened by him and his anger, which she sensed was even deeper than he let on, deeper and hotter and denser. She was most certainly frightened by the gun. And yet she envied him. He had someone to blame, and that seemed to simplify things. If someone shot you, you got to be mad. If you were Bob Wickett and you were mad, you meant to get even with a gun in your hand. If she was going to get a gun and go out for revenge, who would she shoot? Herself? She laughed, then wondered if the very blood that had saved her life might someday become her enemy and kill her. Even if she never had another AVM, her blood might now be spiked with AIDS. There was always that possibility. And who would she shoot for that? Sheila drove toward Maplewood, but her thoughts traveled in several directions at once. She didn't feel the bumps on the road, didn't attend to the rights and lefts.

Bob Wickett had his rage but he had that boy, too. When she told him about her emptiness, he shook his head in pity. No, he didn't feel that, he said. He had love. He loved his boy all the way. Envy visited her again. Someone to blame. Someone to love. All of a sudden she wanted all the work a kid was, and all the love, and she shocked herself. She had been dead certain that children were not her cup of tedium and now she was neither dead nor certain.

Sheila raced through a yellow light. Didn't want to stop. She asked herself, *Why?* But the question didn't fit. What difference did it make? She tried, *What?* What was Bob? A warning. An inspiration. A man with a scar, with lava in his veins. What was she supposed to do? Nothing? Something? Again, she searched for reasons. There was something else. Beyond reason. Rage, love: She was possessed of neither. She was rich in confusion. Loaded. She wanted order. She thought about her list.

Do good.

Do good? What was good? How did you do it? And what did it have to do with driving to Bob Wickett's exact street address accidentally on purpose?

Doctor Hallerman's nurse tapped a chart on her desk as Sheila walked through the door. "How are we?" she asked.

"On time this time," said Sheila.

"No trouble?"

Sheila couldn't bring herself to answer.

"Good!" warbled the nurse.

Trying to escape her roiling mind, Sheila conjured the memory of Hallerman's eyes and reapplied her lipstick in the waiting room. It wasn't that easy. Her chest ached. Her stomach ached. She distracted herself with dreams about Hallerman. His eyes meant life to her, and she loved him with no reserve. How could I not? she wondered. Sheila waited. What was she supposed to do? Nothing came to mind. No one came and offered her an insight, nicely packaged. But she wanted to know. She asked and she meant it. She asked and she wondered and she squirmed, and though she'd not intended any such thing at all, somewhere in the answerless waiting and distress, she felt a certain tenderness emerging, rising from the sucking vortex of her questions. What was it? It made her heart ache, but not unpleasantly. It was new. It was as real as the weather. Depending on your point of view, you might call that newborn tenderness, that lovely human ache, her soul. Up to you, what you call it. That's what it looked like from my point of view. The heavens, the air, the light, the quarks and atoms, rejoiced on her behalf. Meanwhile, she restlessly turned the pages of a magazine, breathing the overheated waiting room air. She waited.

And what about Hallerman? Nothing. At noon, he had been called for emergency surgery. Saving another life. Another and another and another, fumed Sheila, as if this were not a marvel but a form of promiscuity. Was he done with her now that she was alive? He was *her* Hallerman. Her lifesaver. She searched her mind. Wasn't there some kind of ancient tradition in some kind of culture, where the one who saved your life was responsible for it? Wasn't there? She wanted an answer. She answered herself. Yes. She was sure of it, but she wasn't sure where. Wherever it was where the world worked that way, Hallerman was elsewhere. She was on her own. Now what? Sheila struggled into an open-backed examination gown. The nurse reappeared and said, "No, dear. You need the opening in the front." So Sheila struggled again. Nothing was in its proper place. Nothing was what it ought to be. And she couldn't answer her own damn questions to her own satisfaction. Ten minutes later, she was seen and inspected by a woman who called herself Hallerman's associate. Sheila glared at Dr. Jane Wigginham, who had large pores and cold fingers, who spoke quickly and washed her hands and said that Shiela was really healing very well. What would you know? Sheila wanted to say, but at that point she was awhirl in such a divine state of confusion she could barely speak.

From my point of view, she was ripe.

The Seeker and the Sought

Any god will tell you, Confusion can be a wonderful state. Though it is rarely sought, it is often created and from it, the daring, be they earthbound or unseen, can go anywhere. Sheila, when things were stable, was never particularly daring. But as we say in the evolving chaos of eternity, things never change until they change.

And then?

Sheila found it hard to leave her window seat, a condition the confused will recognize. In her case, as she sat, she watched the windows across the road. Watched for the brown face. And never asked herself why her curiosity had grown into preoccupation.

The woman who had captured her attention went by the name Kiri Srinvasar, which was the name her parents had given her. Her home, or at any rate her country of origin, was Sri Lanka, though she tended to think of it as Ceylon, which, as far as the political world was concerned, no longer existed.

Her story is a rather interesting one, and as Miss Kiri Srinvasar was to be the one who set Sheila and her nascent soul on the uncertain path toward Grace and a number of other things, I shall digress for a moment to tell it.

Kiri Srinvasar was a slave. She had not started out that way. She, whose name meant "milky white," had been rather, but not extremely, well born, and unfortunately, a daughter among daughters in a land losing sons, a land at war for too long. Though her mother said that her name came from the fact that she had been as white as Buddha's tooth on the day of her birth, Kiri doubted this was true. She had always known herself to be the color of unpolished copper, a complex brown that was sometimes more red, or haunted by a cloudy gray-green. She had great round black eyes and an uneroded newness to her skin. I do not know her age and I am not sure she knew it. Being who she was, she would have lied and chosen whatever number she wanted in any case. The truth, as you in the Western Hemisphere are bound to call matters perceived to be of irrefutable certainty, was of little interest to her. Nor was I. Kiri had her own very particular interpretation of that which was sublime and that which was divine and that which was neither. She was disposed to create deities as the need arose and was inclined to think she herself had more divine potential than most. More on that as we progress.

Kiri's enslavement came as a surprise to her. Her father, being dead, could not provide. Her mother had decided that of all the daughters, Kiri was most fit to look for work, paying work, so that their difficult circumstances might be relieved. With the help of an aunt on her mother's side, Kiri had gone to Colombo to seek such work. There she had been introduced to a Christian gentleman who engaged young women for what he called situations abroad. He made much of his own kindness and of the expense involved in procuring a desirable post. Kiri and her family had long since lost the resources to even dream of affording his fee or the travel by air, even with the anticipation of a tremendous return on their investment. Happily, or so it seemed at the time, the Christian gentleman had a financing plan that would eliminate all problems. Kiri and her family were made to thoroughly understand the magnitude of their debt and his generosity. He would get her where she was going and delay payment of his fee and then, for ten months, most of Kiri's salary would be sent directly from the employer to him. The debt would be erased in virtually no time with no effort or worry about finances and figuring. Ten months would pass in a wink, and after that, Kiri's pay would be hers without encumbrance and she could send money home directly to her family. Simple.

The Christian gentleman found a place for Kiri in Kuwait, a modern, wealthy country, where she would live in a beautiful mansion and attend the children of a family with royal blood. It was a privilege and a tribute to her qualifications, not to mention the genius of the Christian gentleman, that Kiri should recieve such a precious opportunity. Kiri knew she would be lonely for her village and her mother and her four sisters, but she was happy and the world suddenly seemed big and full of possibility. At night, she began to dream magnificent and magical dreams, so extremely grand that she dared not repeat them even to the sister who shared her bed.

The day she arrived in Kuwait, the mistress took her passport away and hid it for safekeeping, and Kiri was put to work. She had no time even to weep. Work stopped only when she was permitted to sleep. She had no time to see more of her new world than could be seen as the sun rose out the kitchen window. She was not sent to market or allowed to wander. She could not speak Arabic. The children pulled her hair and kicked her when she did not understand. She only liked Anna Maria, the Filipina cook. They chatted when they could, in close-enough versions of grammar school English. Anna Maria told Kiri she was lucky compared to other girls. Some were raped by the sons. Some were whipped with electrical cords and made to sleep on tile floors. She was lucky. Mrs. Babahani was an educated woman who also spoke English, having been to Oxford, and rarely beat her. Kiri had never considered luck in this way. She thought often of writing her family and pleading for their help, for her freedom, but she could not bear to do it and she did not think that she would be believed. She did not believe it herself. She was ashamed and she was tired. At night, her magnificent dreams were replaced by a few hours of dark and desperately welcome oblivion, from which she awakened with dread.

And her debt to the Christian gentleman never seemed to be repaid. After ten months had passed three times, she dared to ask Mrs. Babahani when the day of full repayment would come and she would see her salary. Mrs. Babahani slapped her face with a wet hand.

By Mrs. Babahani's calculation, she did not owe Kiri any payment at all. If anything, the impertinent, untrustworthy girl was more in her debt than she knew. She ate. And food cost money. She slept on a cot. Surely she owed rent. She freely wasted sponges and bleach and pinched sugar for her tea. That was no secret. She owed for that.

On the days when Kiri cleaned in relative solitude, she also searched for her passport. She dug through cabinets and drawers. She looked under mattresses and cushions without success. In frustration, she imagined herself running out the door, empty-handed, no passport, no money, into the street. She could not imagine what would happen next. Without her passport, she could go nowhere and there was nowhere to go.

Late one night, Mrs. Babahani came to her while she was ironing. Her employer stood too long in silence, watching her work. Kiri was afraid. She held a hot iron. That was her protection. She burned her hand as she turned a sleeve. She dared not gasp. Mrs. Babahani saw the burn. "You'll want ice for that," she advised, but then she continued to speak so that Kiri could not go into the kitchen. She told Kiri that the family was going to the United States of America. Her husband had been appointed to a post at the United Nations. She said that if Kiri wished to accompany them, an arrangement could be made. If she did not want to go, a position would be found with another family in Kuwait, in which case she would owe a fee for the trouble of finding such a place and all existing debts would be transferred. Kiri dared to ask if she might go home to Sri Lanka. That she could not do, said Mrs. Babahani, for she still owed interest.

"What interest is this?" Kiri asked.

"Don't test me," growled Mrs. Babahani. Kiri did not test her.

Anna Maria chose to stay behind, and so Kiri sat alone in economy class to London. She feasted on a meal brought to her seat by a beautiful serving woman who generously offered her endless drinks of Coca-Cola with ice. She feasted again as she rode through the clouds from London to JFK and watched an American movie.

Kiri held her passport just long enough to legally enter the United States of America, land of the free. Noting her A-3 servant's visa, the Customs agent cleared his throat and sternly announced where her freedom began and ended: "You realize that if for any reason you leave your current employ, your A-three status will immediately terminate and you will hence be identified as an undocumented, a.k.a. illegal, alien subject to the initiation of deportation proceedings by the INS?"

Kiri nodded her head many times, though she had no idea what he was talking about in these long words. "Yes, yes, sir. Very good, sir. Oh, yes! So true."

The Customs agent smiled and thought, They're always so polite. "Enjoy!" he said vigorously.

"Yes, sir!" she answered, trying to assure him of her obedience. No one had ever ordered her to enjoy anything, certainly not the uniformed agent of a foreign power. What would happen if she did not? She resolved to obey, considering these orders to be a clear sign auguring the pleasurable future. Enjoy. Her coat was all of a sudden so warm that she found it difficult to get enough air. There was no time to take it off, so she sat in sweat. Kiri was no longer sure what enjoying might be and could not help wondering at the consequences of failure.

But she forgot her orders and her worry soon enough.

Her passport was taken away from her in the car. Her duties resumed the minute the limousine pulled up to the Babahanis' new house on Currier Street. Only there was more to do and there was no one to talk to because Anna Maria had stayed behind. Kiri was not permitted to speak to the man who mowed the lawn. She was to accept the groceries from the delivery truck with a thank-you and no more.

Sheila knew none of this. Though she felt sadness as she stared at the brown face, she was not sure whose sadness it was. Staring across the street at a distance of hundreds of feet, the brown face was nearly featureless in miniature. Sheila didn't even try to imagine the eyes, the nose, the mouth. From the way the brown-faced woman had run from the sound of her mistress's Miata, Sheila sensed Kiri's fear. She sensed enclosure, even captivity, but these were not ideas she put into words, even in her own mind. She just watched, and in the watching found respite from the strain of her own captivity. She was still aching, imprisoned in her mind and discomfort, exhausted from her splattered efforts to force herself to actually *Know* What to Do so she could get on with it. But as you have no doubt noticed yourself, confusion will not be rushed, and neither will knowing.

It seemed to Sheila that the children across the street watched TV from after school to bedtime. What she couldn't know was how grateful Kiri was that they did. It was on the TV that Kiri saw America. She saw handsome cops with guns, and game shows and yellow-haired women who all looked the same, sometimes weeping, sometimes drinking, sometimes having sex in the afternoon. She could not stop and stand and stare. Whatever she saw, she saw in bits as she dusted the set, mopped the floor, polished the furniture. She never saw slaves. Hearing TV, which was in English, made her feel less a stranger. She liked English as well as her native Sinhalese, maybe better. The language of Kuwait had always seemed strange to her, hissing and throaty, hostile, wicked. Though they spoke English at school, the Babahani children did not speak it at home. Their orders were still given in Arabic. They still kicked her and pulled her hair. Even so, she hated them less than she had, and this was because of their passion for American television. Were it not for their hours of TV watching, she would not have learned the companionable jingles that circled her mind all day as she worked, and how would she have seen the wonder of common men and women winning big fortunes, thousands or millions of dollars, every Wednesday? If she ever again left the Babahani house, escaped, was somehow free, Kiri knew what she wanted to do. She wanted to go to the place where she could win Lotto. Over and over the TV assured her. Anyone can win it. For the justice and the beauty of this reason alone, Kiri loved Connecticut in the United States America, sight unseen. Kiri wondered if the other slaves in Connecticut, USA, lived as she did. Sometimes she imagined there was a woman somewhere, a secret friend, who knew exactly how Kiri felt, how she craved a day on which she would do nothing but lie in bed, eat chocolate-covered biscuits, and drink Ceylonese tea.

And Then

One day, when the damp burrowed into Sheila's scar
and weakened her with pain that had the throbbing
rhythm of a heartbeat, when the silence, the solitude
made her feel like she was a ghost, mistaken about her own
survival, no longer a part of this world, one day as she yearned
for the phone to ring and interrupt itself and ring again, for
demands and decisions that had to be made, for no time to eat
or sleep or stare out the same single window for hours and
hours and hours, one day, Sheila saw the brown-faced woman
standing coatless on the lawn. She was crying.

As if she had been summoned, Sheila rose, and ignoring her
pain, she draped a green mohair shawl over her shoulder. Without thinking whether she ought or ought not, whether she'd be
welcomed or shunned, Sheila sidled down the stairs, resting her
weight on the banister, using the strength of her arms to speed
her downward. She hobbled across the street, unable to run,
which was just as well. If Kiri had seen someone running toward
her, she would, without doubt, have run away.

"Is everything all right?" Sheila called, waving her hand.

"Fine. Fine," answered Kiri, startled at the stranger's inquiry. "Fine fine fine."

Sheila stared at Kiri as if her childlike beauty were a compelling and grotesque deformity. She had expected an old woman. She reached in a pocket, pulled out a crumpled tissue, and offered it. "It's clean," she said.

Kiri accepted the tissue and stepped back away from the panting white woman who had appeared from nowhere. "Yes, yes. Of course."

Sheila saw Kiri's cracked hands and gnarled, bleeding knuckles. "Is there something wrong?"

"No no no no no," insisted Kiri. She hid her hands behind her back, but the wind forced her to expose her hands again. She crossed her arms and tucked them at the sides of her breasts like two birds seeking shelter.

Sheila pointed up and across the street. "I live there. My name is Sheila. If you need help . . ." she repeated.

"Oh, I am fine. Very very very fine," insisted Kiri. And then she changed her mind. The night before, the eldest boy had placed a hand on her breast, and where that hand had rested, she felt shame entering her body. The night before, the eldest boy had given her sticky socks to wash and laughed in a predatory way. What was she to do? Not a thing. Nothing. Nothing. But if she took a chance and spoke to this woman? If she took a chance and it was the wrong chance, there would be a terrible beating perhaps. Or something worse. If she did not take a chance, this chance that had come to find her, there might never be another. "You will help?" she began tentatively.

As Sheila nodded, she was suddenly pierced by a spear of apprehension. What might *yes* mean? She dismissed the question from her mind. "Yes," she said.

Ripeness

I mentioned that Sheila was ripe. But unlike the usual fruit, she had more to do than dangle, fall, and be devoured. Now that she was off the vine, she sought meaning, and in order to find it, she had harvesting of her own to do.

Kiri was her juicy strawberry, her blushing apple, her waiting peach, her ready golden pear, ready to be grasped and savored. But Kiri had not appeared crying on the lawn so Sheila could conveniently end her captivity. Oh no.

What sent Kiri to the lawn that day in tears was not an impulse toward freedom or some new and special grief but the eye-burning spray of a large white onion.

In her rush to relieve the sting with fresh air, she had left uncovered chicken on the kitchen counter. As she told Sheila of her enslavement, she worried. The cat might already have the chicken between her paws. And the little girl was due off the school bus in minutes. If the child saw Sheila—disaster! She would surely tattle to her mother and there would be terrible trouble.

Sheila agreed. "We can't let them see me." Her gaze followed Kiri's down the driveway. It wasn't far. "Can you run now?"

"Run?" If she ran, it would have to be without her passport. The Mrs. had hidden it well. As she cleaned, Kiri had searched. She had even found the place where Mistress's diamonds were cached, but not her own passport. She would have to run without it. But she could not simply run. There was a photograph of her family—Kiri and her sisters, children, all barefoot, squeezed chest to back so that no one would be left out of the frame, her ring-eyed father, young there, her mother, pregnant and tired with her braid falling over her swollen breast. It was hidden in the pantry. She could not run without that. There was a wooden comb her father had carved for her mother before their marriage, and a small filigreed metal box that had belonged to her great-grandmother. She could not run without that. In the downstairs toilet tank nearest her cot, she had hidden a thread-thin gold bracelet given her, with great hopes, by her aunt, who had worn it on her wedding day. She could not leave, she could not live, without those.

"Can you hurry and get them?"

"There is no time," Kiri protested.

Sheila could not understand her hesitation. This was freedom she was offering. "Go!"

Kiri ran into the house. She fished her aunt's wedding bracelet from the toilet. Ran to the basement to retrieve her few heirlooms from behind the boiler. Ran to the pantry. Grabbed the photograph. Ran past the purring cat, who had the chicken on the floor. She ran to the front porch.

There was no Sheila.

She saw a yellow school bus at the foot of the driveway. She did not step off the porch. She did not look to see where Sheila had gone. What did it matter? she thought to herself, feeling a troubling sense of relief. Gone was gone.

Kiri returned to the kitchen with dry eyes. She allowed the

cat to continue her bloody feast as she stowed her treasures behind the Comet and the Dash. Then she picked what was left of the gnawed chicken up off the floor and cubed it.

"I'm hungry," whined the little girl as she threw her book bag on the table.

Kiri tossed the onion and the cubes of chicken together in a pot on the stove and lit a low flame under the Babahanis' dinner. She added coriander, cumin, cinnamon, and nutmeg, and when the scent was right, she bathed the sizzling mix in a half pint of cream. She washed her hands and smiled at the child. "Yes, yes. Some apple. How would you like some very good healthy apple perhaps?"

"I want a cookie."

"A cookie. Of course."

She waited until she heard the music from the television and then she allowed herself the painful freedom of a thought. Perhaps the woman Sheila would come to her again. No, she thought. Twice was not possible. Why, then, had she come at all, even once? Teased her with hope, stirred her awareness of the possibility that she might escape to a new life, and then vanished?

By the time the Babahani family sat down together to enjoy their evening meal in the main dining room, Kiri was no longer certain that the white woman who called herself Sheila was a mortal being. She might have been a godly messenger for good or evil yet to come. If that was the case, what did the Sheila mean and what was her true provenance? Why had she worn green? Why were her fingernails red? Why was she not radiant and powerful, but sickly, wan, and frail? These questions took Kiri so far away from the place where she stood that the Mrs. felt forced to slap her once with the front of her hand and once with the back, scoring Kiri's cheek with a bloody scratch from the elevated prongs of a diamond cocktail ring.

"I said *move*, you little stupid. We need more chicken here sometime today *if* you can manage to perform this great and enormous kindness before we all starve waiting."

The children laughed.

"And wipe your face, Miss Piggy. Must we look at that?"

Kiri wiped her sleeve across her face, leaving an unsightly red streak. "Oh God," said the oldest boy.

Mrs. Babahani set down her fork and looked at her son in shock. "I will not hear such language."

"Enough!" shouted Mr. Babahani. "If I cannot have peace while I eat, I will dine alone."

Kiri dipped the silver spoon into the rice and made a perfect mound on her mistress's plate. Then she dipped the ladle into the uncovered tureen and poured the curried chicken stew so that the sauce spread over the rice in the shape of a star.

Sheila's Debt

W hen the school bus dropped the Babahani girl at the foot of the driveway, Sheila hid behind a tree. She saw Kiri at the porch but did not call to her. She couldn't. It was too late. The girl would hear. The girl would see. And then there would be no chance at a second chance. As soon as Kiri returned to the house, Sheila crept away, angry at herself and even angrier at Kiri for not seizing her moment. What was so important that it could not be left behind when freedom called?

Because Kiri had hesitated to run, Sheila tried to doubt what she had told her. It was preposterous. Perhaps she was lying. This is America, Sheila said to herself, but even as she said it, she half remembered tales of Mexicans who had been enslaved in California for the purpose of picking thorned and fragrant roses. And remembering the Mexicans helped her recall some story she had heard or read about indentured Chinese refugees who had been forced to work in dress factories to pay back the enormous price of their passage from China to New York.

If Sheila did not quite know how to wholeheartedly believe

Kiri's story, neither could she wholeheartedly doubt it. It bore all the marks of truth. It was told with too much resignation, too little living spirit to be a lie. Kiri was a woman so in debt as to be indentured until her life had no more value to her creditors. What she owed was unclear, but whatever it was, whether or not it was actually anything at all, Kiri, and now Sheila, knew it could never be satisfactorily repaid. Kiri was a slave and a broken soul. Sheila now knew one other thing. Kiri would never leave the Babahanis by herself. She did not need debt to keep her captive anymore; habit would do. If Kiri had been the kind who could seize her own freedom, grab it like a wanton clump of daylilies by the side of the road, it would already be hers.

It was up to Sheila to make Kiri free. That was what she decided. The day's mishap had given her time to think, and that was good. She thought about the Ellens, strangers who had so recently stood beside her, cleaned away her runny shit and her endless blood, strangers who held her swollen hands as she was dying. She owed them, them and Hallerman, Kiri's freedom. Although she had just failed to obtain it, Sheila was suddenly happy. Goodness seemed less of an abstraction. It seemed practically easy. Being a better person, being happy—these things, she concluded, had to do with the brown-faced stranger named Kiri Srinvasar. She felt it was her duty as an American, if not her destiny as a human, to free this particular slave, give her her life back, see her torn hands heal. She set about planning Kiri's (and she could not help suspecting her own) emancipation.

Sheila sat at the same window and saw what she had seen before, but now she had a purpose. For several days she studied the comings and goings of the Babahani family. The father always left first. A black-windowed Jaguar came to fetch him at 7:15 each morning. A uniformed chauffeur would hold the door. After that, the children would go. The bus that came for the little girl stopped at the foot of the driveway at 7:45. The boy waited with her and then caught his own bus at the end of the block. The mother waved from the porch but never left it. Usually, she retreated inside the house until about 9:30. Then Kiri would place a black nylon bag in the backseat of the red Miata and the Mrs., who was so extraordinarily chic that Sheila could not help but await her appearance with both curiosity and excitement, would ride off. Her return was somewhat unpredictable, but never before one in the afternoon. The groceries came on Tuesdays and Thursdays. The dry cleaner delivered on Fridays. Wednesday was the day when Kiri was alone in the house for the longest period of time.

Sheila never asked herself whether what she was planning was the right thing. Of that, she had no doubt. She waited for the soonest Wednesday, unable to think of anything but the Moment. She prayed, though not specifically to me, for luck. This, I determined to grant her, though not necessarily in a form or from an angle she would readily indentify. And so, most certainly, luck was hers, metaphysically speaking. But then, what luck is not metaphysical?

On the morning of the Wednesday she was waiting for, three weeks after her first attempt, the Jaguar limousine came on time despite freezing rain. School was delayed an hour, which made both the buses accordingly late, but once the children were gone, so was their mother, in her glistening red Miata. As Sheila tied back her hair, she wondered, for the first time, where Mrs. Babahani went. Surely not to work. Perhaps to shop. Perhaps to a lover. Perhaps both. Sheila waited until the car could neither be heard nor seen, and then she waited to be sure no one returned.

Though her observations were precise, and there was little need for precaution, Sheila did not want to fail twice. Sheila tucked her hair into a wooly hat and grabbed a pair of oversize sunglasses some volunteer had left behind at Coxx headquarters. They hid most of her face. Dressed in overalls and a heavy sweater that added bulk, she drove north to Warrington Center and rented a van that resembled the one from Qwik Kleen. Then she stopped at the florist and bought a large bouquet of mixed red flowers. That way, if there should be anyone else at the house, she could simply drive up, deliver the flowers, and leave. If the neighbors peeked out their windows, they would see a van much like the vans that dropped off their shirts and their flowers, their milk and their Quaker Oatmeal. Nothing odd.

Sheila parked to the side of the Babahanis' house in the same spot where delivery vans parked. She rang the bell at the kitchen door. Kiri did not come. She was cleaning grout from the tiles in the Mrs.' upstairs bath. Sheila poked the black button and held it so the buzz would be heard anywhere in the house. Heavy feet pounded down wooden stairs. Heavier steps than she would have expected. She squeezed the bouquet and stepped back from the door. Kiri opened it. She smelled of noxious foam cleanser. She did not look at Sheila's face. She reached for the flowers. Not knowing what else to do, Sheila handed them to her.

"Thank you," said Kiri, pulling the door closed.

"Wait. It's me. Sheila from across the street."

"Ah! Sheila who will help. Very good."

"How long will it take you to get ready?"

"Ready, Miss?"

"To go. To get out of here."

"Out of here?"

Sheila sighed impatiently. "Escape."

"Oh, yes yes. Yes, you. Very good." Kiri tried to shut the door again, but Sheila's shoe blocked it. Kiri pushed. She had learned from the last time. The door would not close. She refused to imagine freedom coming so neatly to collect her. Escape. Though she had imagined it for years in pieces and wisps, when presented, it seemed like foolishness. The whole business. Who knew what it would mean? Escape. The word sounded wrong as she thought it. She could not just walk out the door. To what? And then? "Escape," she said. "I do not think so. Thank you very much. Good-bye."

Sheila dismissed her refusal entirely. "Get your things," she commanded. "Where are your things?"

"In the pantry, Miss."

"Well, get them. Now! Run!"

Sheila sounded like the Mrs., sharp and in no mood for disobedience, so Kiri obeyed, as she knew she was expected to do. She shoved her treasures into a Stop & Shop bag.

"Is there anything else? Where's your coat?"

"No coat, Miss."

"No coat." Sheila considered this. "Be sure you haven't taken anything that's not yours. I don't want them . . ."

Kiri began to cry and embraced the shopping bag as if it were a helpless baby.

Sheila reached out and pushed Kiri's detergent-spattered black hair away from her eyes. "I'm sorry. I didn't mean to accuse. I was just . . ."

"I have not prepared dinner," said Kiri. "I have not prepared . . ." The phone began to ring.

"Let's go!" With one arm around Kiri's shoulder, Sheila steered the shivering woman to the passenger seat of the van. "Stay down until I say."

The red Miata was turning into the drive. "Shit!" Sheila shoved the glasses on and kept her head down. The Mrs.! Why was she here? She was never here at this hour! She contorted her face to make it strange and waved as she pulled to the side to let the Mrs. pass. The Mrs. ignored the van and the wave. She did not wave to tradespeople. Sheila held her breath and checked her rearview mirror. How long did they have until discovery? Minutes at the most. As soon as they turned out of the driveway, she pressed her foot on the gas. "We'll have to hustle," she said. There was no point in telling Kiri how close they'd come. If they were going to be caught . . . Sheila did not want to think of it.

Kiri stayed down as she was told, she stayed down and wept. Hot air blew from the van's vents. She opened her eyes and stared at her chapped knees. Then she clamped her teeth into her arm. Held her flesh in her mouth so she would not scream from fear.

Sheila drove fast for fifteen minutes in silence, still checking the rearview mirror for the Miata, listening to the radio as if it could tell her what she needed to know to be safe. She drove until she felt they were far enough away, going by her gut and not the mileage, then she said, "It's okay. You can sit up now." She tapped Kiri's shoulder and giggled. "Hey, Kiri! We did it! Wow!" Kiri straightened her back but did not raise her head. "Holy moly. We just strolled right on out, la-di-da, easy as easy could be." She sighed again, remembering the Mrs. Thank heaven for hauteur, she thought. What if she'd taken a good look? What if she'd been friendly? But she hadn't. "Just like that." Sheila snapped her fingers. Kiri jumped. "You're totally free! I can't believe it."

"It is not true," Kiri whispered.

"Oh yes, it is. Totally true."

"The Mrs. will be very very annoyed and angry if I am not being in the house to make it clean and I am gone at dinner."

"Well, the hell with the Mrs."

Kiri thought about that. Would such words be spoken if she were not free? "I am free," she declared tentatively. She had been not free, she reasoned. So why could she not now be free? "Oh yes, Miss. The absolutely utterly hell with the Mrs. then, as you say. Yes yes."

Sheila laughed again. Kiri had not laughed in such a long time. She screeched like a seagull until she could not breathe.

She inhaled and cawed. That was her laughter. And then it came more easily. She copied Sheila's sounds, and out came a free and lovely laugh. This became her laugh, her first possession as a free woman, and Kiri and Sheila laughed the same, freely, together in great happiness as they rode to the rental place to return the van.

Sheila thought nothing of the pain that so much laughing caused along her scar. It was there, a tearing feeling as her body shook with glee, but she did not care to think about it. Sheila and Kiri laughed and laughed, and for a short time, that was all either woman could have wanted.

Paradise Found

T hough Sheila had never freed a slave before, she felt
she could make a few assumptions. Like: Anyone who
had been inclined to enslave another person would be
furious about losing the free labor. Sheila could not know what
the Babahanis would do about their loss, but she could assume
they'd be likely to search, at least for a while, before bringing
in some new unfortunate. She doubted they'd call in the cops.
It was hard to picture a sympathetic reaction from the burly,
beer-drinking Fallowfield police when they learned that the
local bandits in bedsheets, which was how they privately re-
ferred to the Babahanis, had a runaway-slave problem. On the
other hand, outrage is an awfully extravagant and unpredictable creature. If the Mr. and Mrs. truly saw Kiri as their personal
property, they just might be indignant enough to risk an international incident to get her back. Sheila made two other assumptions. One, they would lie. The last thing they'd do was
fess up to being slaveholders. They could easily tell the cops
their maid had stolen their silver and fled. And two, there was
virtually no way to connect Sheila Jericault with any of this

unless the Mrs. had an unexpectedly good eye.

That didn't mean Sheila and Kiri could be careless. As far as Sheila was concerned, they were on the lam. At least temporarily. She had parked her car at Avis so that as soon as the van was returned, they could take off. Within two hours, they reached their destination, a spot that Kiri immediately understood to be an earthly paradise.

She asked herself what in her unremembered past lives and her unrevealed destiny caused her to suddenly be transported from debt and abominable slavery to a beautiful room in a modern palace known as the Marriott, a room with two wide, soft beds, a giant television, a clean white bathroom with white towels and white terry robes and two sets of packaged miniature soaps and lotions and shampoos. She did not know how to begin to question the turn in her fate, so she deliberately put the wondering aside lest the business of wondering itself sully the unfolding. What was, was. And the meaning? She expected that when it was ready to reveal itself, and she was ready to know, it would be be made plain.

Meanwhile, she marveled at the Marriott. Even the uniformed servants who passed in the halls were smiling.

"Why don't you take a shower and freshen up?" said Sheila as she lay back on one of the beds to rest.

Kiri showered for a long time, as long as she wished and then longer just because she was free and she could shower as long as the Mrs. if that was what pleased her. When her fingers were prunish and she had exhausted her every reason and desire to be pummeled by hot water, she annointed herself with pink lotion that made her smell like a sweet spiced cake.

She wrapped her hair in a white towel and enveloped her body in a white robe. The terry tickled the top of her toes. She bent down. The clothes she had been wearing when she fled were not on the floor where she'd put them. She was not sad or even surprised to see them gone. Why should she be surprised? It was right that they should vanish here in the paradise of Marriott on this extraordinary day.

Sheila waited for her beside a table set for two. There was a red rose at the center of the table, which was covered with silver trays. French toast. Eggs. Bacon. Coffee. Orange juice. Milk. And Sheila said, "A celebration. You must be starved."

Kiri did not know what to do. She had not dined at a table in years. After the Babahanis were done and she had cleared their plates, she was permitted to eat what they had not finished, standing, in the kitchen, alone.

"Sit. Eat," said Sheila.

Kiri did so. She watched Sheila and ate what she ate, careful to take the same amount or less. She did not want to offend. "Very very good," she said. "Very very many thanks for this freedom. Yes."

"It is my pleasure. It really is." It really was. Sheila stood and Kiri stood. "No. Sit. Finish. Eat as much as you want." Sheila waited for Kiri to seat herself and smiled as if something great had been accomplished. "Would you be afraid if I left you here for an hour or so? You could put on the TV." Sheila placed the remote control on the table.

"I would not be afraid." As I said, Kiri had decided that she must place her faith in the unnamed but powerful divinities who had suddenly begun to direct their vastly abundant good-will toward her. But not entirely. "You will come back?"

"In a very short time."

Kiri watched a woman in red eyeglasses who brought to-gether a woman and her sister who had not spoken to her since the husband of one became the husband of the other. The women wept and then they laughed, and when a man appeared on the stage where they sat, one of the women removed her shoe and threw it at his head, and Kiri laughed at that. She moved to one of the wide beds and lay down on the flowered spread with her back against three soft pillows and her bare feet up on another. Like a goddess, she thought, a goddess at rest on the highest and most sacred peak. On the table between the beds, she placed her coffee. And she picked it up and sipped it and put it down when she wanted to as many times as she wanted to. When it was gone, she poured herself more from a silver pot.

Sheila returned with many packages. In the packages were all new clothes. "I think these will fit," said Sheila.

Kiri and the packages disappeared into the bathroom. She pulled a white cotton turtleneck over her head and over that, a heavy red sweater. She opened another package and found a plastic tube filled with three balls of fabric. What were these? She pulled open the white lid sealing the tube and pushed the balls out onto the bath mat. Panties. In pink, turquoise, and candy stripes. Three pairs. A choice. She chose the stripes. Another bag. Trousers. Black corduroy trousers. She touched her cheek to the softness. "Lovely lovely things," she murmured prayerfully. The trousers on, she chose again. There were two pairs of socks. Red and black. Red it was. And she looked at herself in the mirror, lifting one foot and then the other and finally climbing onto the counter so she could see the whole effect, head to toe, relying on the reflection to prove her bounty real. Finally, she remembered Sheila. She stepped out and turned, modeling her clothing like a practiced game-show hostess.

Sheila clapped her hands. "You are a vision!"

"I am a radiant vision of beauty in such excellent clothes of my finest dreams," said Kiri to her benefactress.

Sheila laughed with joy. Kiri's unhampered delight delighted Sheila more than she might ever have imagined. This was better than winning some damned election. When had she been so simply happy? "And here," she said, excited. "This is yours, too!" She handed Kiri a hunter green parka with a brown rabbit-fur ruff around the hood. Kiri hugged it as if it were her dearest friend. "Try it on." Kiri wiggled into the parka, pulling the ruff tight around her face. "Perfect!" Sheila watched as Kiri's fingers stroked the fur, and suddenly her pleasure was muddled by queasiness. She breathed deeply, in, then out, to calm the nausea with cool air. Her attention had settled on the horrible torn, peeling skin on Kiri's hands and the ragged gash where the Mrs.' diamond had scored her cheek. There were certain things new clothes could not disguise. Kiri giggled. She had found the drawstring that could draw the parka in about her waist. "Nice," said Sheila. The scars would heal. The uneven timidity of Kiri's glance, her slope-shouldered posture, her weighted stance of burden-bearing defeat, would surely all blow away like clouds in a windy sky as Kiri came to know and trust that she was captive no more. Sheila could think of nothing more worthy than being the one to acquaint Miss Kiri Srinvasar with her freedom. She pictured herself as the all-generous sun bestowing warmth, making life possible, causing this frail flower of the Orient, for this is what she wrongly imagined Kiri to be, to open its petals toward her, revealing never-before-seen colors as it unfurled. She thought neither of dark centers nor the thirst of such a plant, but it was early yet, and from Sheila's point of view, having any purpose that she could define as good was purpose enough. "I think we'll stay here for a couple of days, relax, this and that. If ever there were two people who deserved a break . . . And anyway, it's best to . . ." Sheila stopped. She did not want to load Kiri with new fears and worries, but she had to say something. "Just in case, just for safety's sake, if anyone asks, you're an old friend of mine. Of my family. From India. Say from India, okay? And now you live in . . . Never mind. Just that you're my old family friend."

"Oh yes indeed," said Kiri. "I will be very very happy that you are my very good friend indeed to whom I am most grateful."

Sheila had forgotten to get Kiri a pair of shoes and certainly the flip-flops in which she had made her escape would never do, but Sheila decided precaution came first. She stuffed toilet paper in the toes of her red size 7 sneakers, and Kiri slid them onto her tiny feet, tying the laces as tight as they would go. Kiri stumbled to the elevator, picking up each foot as if it belonged to a stranger, relearning the business of walking, but by the time they got to the beauty salon in the lobby, her gait seemed almost natural. As soon as she walked through the door, the beauticians gathered around, and it would not have mattered if Kiri had been wearing duck feet. So black was her hair, so shiny, so long, so straight and thick. "Stunning," sighed the receptionist, and the women in the salon, the manicurists, the shampooers, the cutters, and the customers echoed, "Stunning." Sheila smiled and Kiri smiled, neither of them knowing what to do next. "Um, actually, we were hoping for maybe a cut and perm," said Sheila, wincing as she anticipated the response.

"Oh no!" cried the receptionist.

Sheila held up one finger, and with it gestured a request for private audience. The receptionist stepped out from behind her ornately carved desk and leaned toward Sheila to hear her whispered explanation. "She's just been through the most horrendous breakup. Real creep. And I mean the worst. She needs a new look to lift her spirits."

The receptionist nodded. That changed everything. She put an arm around Kiri's shoulder. "We'll take good care of you, honey," she said to Kiri. "You just come right along with Val." Val looked at the scab that marred Kiri's perfect cheek and shook her head. "I been there," she said kindly. "You're gonna be just fine. The main thing is, Don't let 'em lure you back. No matter what. Don't go back."

"Never never," said Kiri.

Kiri sat in the padded vinyl chair and let her hair be washed. She felt the gentle hands at her scalp and closed her eyes in joyful surrender. Two hours later, she looked at herself and saw chin-length curls. She stared at the stranger in the mirror, waiting for her to say something, to break into a jingle perhaps, for she, Kiri, Kiri the slave, had become like one of the perfect television women. How splendid she looked to her own eyes. How could there be so many wonders on one earth in one life? She touched her hair carefully. It still felt like hair. She pulled at it. It was hers. The curls were her curls. "Ah . . ." Kiri sighed. She had no words for her pleasure.

Sheila was less happy. She wasn't sure she liked the change at all. It was necessary, yes. Absolutely essential for the sake of Kiri's continued freedom. But something of Kiri's alien delicacy seemed to have fallen to the mock-tile linoleum floor. "It *completely* brings out your eyes," crooned Sheila, when no other praise came to mind.

Kiri just watched the mirror. The receptionist came over to admire. Inspired, she chose a lipstick from the cosmetic display. She softened Kiri's chapped lips with an almond-flavored paste and then painted her mouth a shocking poppy red. "There you go," she said soothingly. "And perhaps a soft romantic charcoal liner for evening . . ."

Kiri issued unending, overflowing thank-yous. Sheila paid the bill with her charge card and guided Kiri by the elbow out the door to the car. Kiri stared at herself in the side mirror and hummed the tune to a Wheaties commercial as they drove to a Mobil station. There, Sheila got gas and checked the oil, and Kiri realized a dream that had just that morning seemed more real and meaningful to her than freedom itself. Sheila gave her a dollar and she, Kiri Srinvasar, bought and paid for a scratch-away instant Lotto ticket.

"And now I am winning the big cash prize," announced Kiri as if no other possibility existed.

"Well . . ." Sheila dug for a penny in her purse. "It doesn't really work that way. There's a thing called odds. And it's like

for every one ticket you buy, you have something like five million chances you won't win. And only one that you will." Sheila
handed Kiri the coin. She would have to learn sooner or later.
"Scratch the black away," Sheila instructed. Kiri scoured the
five black boxes on her ticket until there was no more black.
She handed the ticket to Sheila.

"And so?"

"So it's a serious waste of money if you calculate the other
useful ways you might spend a hard-earned dollar." Sheila
glanced at the ticket. Kiri had won a thousand dollars cash.
"Oh my God!" she shouted, though I have nothing to do with
human games of chance. "Sir!" Sheila dashed to the cash register and interrupted the teenage boy behind the counter. He
held up his hand, signaling them to wait. He was mumbling
into the telephone. She held the Lotto ticket in front of his eyes
and he grabbed it.

"Whoa . . . Holy shit!" he shouted. "Later." He hung up the
phone.

"So what happens now?" said Sheila. Kiri was clutching herself so that her fingers were buried deep in her sweater.

"Is it yours?"

"It's hers."

"Well then, she fills out the back and we give her a grand in
pure cash money."

"You won!" marveled Sheila, feeling blessed on Kiri's behalf.
"I never knew anyone who ever won more than five bucks."

"The most we had in here was a hundred." He pointed to
the see-though Plexiglas wall that separated him from his customers. There, a Polaroid picture of a fat, smiling man was
Scotch-taped above the chewing-tobacco dispenser.

Sheila flipped the ticket over and pulled Kiri aside. "You
better let me do the filling out."

"Yes yes. It is proper that the one thousand dollars is truly
yours, for it was your one dollar . . ."

"Forget about that. I never would have bought the ticket. It was your luck, Kiri. Absolutely your very own incredibly good luck. I just don't want him to take your photograph, if you know what I mean." Kiri knew. Sheila filled out the ticket and handed it to the boy. "She's terribly camera-shy."

"Fine by me, but the goverment's going to take their slice," he said.

"What?" Sheila tasted her heart.

"Taxes. You take the money. You pay the taxes. That's how it works."

"Oh. No problem," said Sheila.

"No problem, eh? Hey, maybe you're like some kind of me-gacitizen or something? Like, maybe you wanna pay some of my dad's taxes, too," he said, pulling a camera from the shelf below the register and taking a greenish flash picture before Sheila had a chance to pose. "He owes like twenty grand. The IRS wants to eat him alive, man."

Kiri wanted to hear more about this monster and its whereabouts, but she dared not ask. The boy disappeared into a locked room. Sheila rubbed her eyes. She was still seeing red spots when the boy returned and handed her nine one-hundred-dollar bills and five twenties. Sheila placed the bills in Kiri's hands and closed her fingers around them. "Yours. Congratulations," she said.

"Yeah. Like way major stat on those kind of bucks," said the boy.

"What more of wonder on this day?" said Kiri as she buckled her seat belt.

"Shoes," answered Sheila. "Definitely shoes."

They drove to the Nutmeg Country Mall, which was larger than Kiri's home village. "Goodness gracious to the highest heavens!" Kiri exclaimed as she turned in place, surveying the endless stores and stalls, smelling the aroma of plastic, cinnamon, and perfume in this place where the light belonged neither to the day nor to the night but to its own time, and the convergence of so many human conversations created a new kind of quiet that was as comforting as a waterfall, a quiet of noise.

At the first shoe store they saw, to Kiri's amazement, a salesman knelt before her and politely requested that she place her bare feet on a metal scale, and stand. She looked down on his balding head as he gently pressed her toes to the metal and announced that Kiri was a perfect size 5B, both right and left. With this knowledge, they were able to purchase two very practical pairs of walking shoes, one brown, one black, with almost no bother at all. At the second, Sheila bought Kiri deerskin moccasins adorned with beaded thunderbirds in flight. Now, posessed of three pairs of shoes, it seemed to both Kiri and Sheila that these wonderful shoes called for wonderful socks. On the way to the store that sold wonderful socks, they stopped at Macy's. Again they were fortunate, for on this day, Kiri's first day of freedom, there was also a Fabulous One-Day Sale. Sheila said it was synchronicity, and because of it, they purchased all the dainty lace panties and matching brassieres that Kiri might need for now and into the indefinite future. As they left the lingerie department, they saw the loveliest pair of shearling-lined boots. "It's winter, you'll need boots," said Sheila, and so another pair of 5Bs became Kiri's own. Sheila quite casually asked if they had a similar pair in a 7, and it just so happened that they did. Then Sheila bought Kiri a waterproof watch, a wallet in which to put her new money, and a pair of purple woolly gloves with a matching beret. She bought Kiri a dress and nylon stockings, which led to the obvious need for a pair of 5B high heels. Then Sheila bought herself a woolly blanket, a beautiful goose-down comforter, and another one, plus a pillow, for Kiri. If one had comforters, one needed comforter covers, and so two of these were chosen and bought.

As Sheila went to pay for this last purchase, Kiri said, "Perhaps I shall buy this with my winnings of Lotto money?"

Sheila patted her hand. "No. That's for your future. You save that."

Kiri reached forward somewhat fearfully to touch with her own fingers the gold plastic card that brought forth such endless riches. It felt cool but not cold. Sheila handed it to her. She handed it back quickly, awed, and a bit distrustful of its enormous power. "Is there nothing we cannot buy?" Kiri asked carefully, so that she would not offend.

"Must be something," Sheila laughed. "But not here." She thought for a moment. "Don't you think we ought to get you a nightgown? I think we need some cozy flannel nightgowns. And fuzzy slippers. So our toes don't get a chill."

"Oh yes!" Kiri agreed. "We need that indeed."

This dizzying lust, this expansive need, was, when so easily satisfied, irresistible. Kiri had not known until this day how many things she needed. She had not even known to yearn for such things as a down-filled blanket. It was so easy to learn. Here she had not even dared to need her own freedom and now she needed a new nightgown, maybe more than one, and naturally she needed fuzzy slippers for her toes, and who knew what else she might need? "I need . . ." She tried it out. "I need perhaps . . ."

"A nice, warm terry velour robe!" Sheila finished the thought Kiri had not quite been able to form.

"Yes!" She *did* need that. Now she did. And as she recognized it, yes, she felt that need as physically, as desperately, as she'd so recently felt the need to rest her hands, to rest her body, to have a full night's sleep. "Every single thing in this new life is so extremely very, very excellent!" she declared.

Sheila was tired. Under her scar her body was throbbing and hot, begging her to show mercy and let it rest. She sat on a bench near a fountain with violet water that shot up and down in energetic spurts. "You must be exhausted," said Sheila.

"Not at all, not at all. I am filled with utter liveliness," Kiri answered.

"Well, I'm about ready to fold," said Sheila, hoping that if she closed her eyes for a few moments, saw nothing and said nothing, energy would return to her. She wondered if she ought to explain about the dying and all that, but it didn't seem the right time.

Kiri wandered to the waterside, thinking about socks. She had never seen so many colors and she was glad that Sheila had encouraged her to take all the ones that pleased her. To choose would have been a struggle.

There were silver and copper coins scattered under the purpled water. The shoppers walked by, hardly noticing the money in the fountain, never stopping to pick it up. A mother handed her daughter a dime and stood smiling as the child cast the money away. The mother said, "Good shot, honey!" and tapped her stroller. The little girl climbed in and rolled off toward The Gap. Kiri wondered at the value of her thousand dollars. Perhaps it was so easy to win because the winning of dollars was of little value compared to the plastic card. "Sheila?"

Sheila opened her eyes. "I need a cup of coffee," she said.

"Do you prefer to throw your small bits of money into the water?"

"What?" Kiri pointed to the fountain. Sheila laughed. "Oh, that's just for luck. You throw a penny in and make a wish. Or if you want to come back. Then you throw one in and wish for that." Sheila handed Kiri a penny. Kiri tossed it. "Good shot," said Sheila.

"Do you wish a throw?"

Sheila found another penny and tossed it in, and made an impossible wish to grant. No matter. That which you do *not* wish for is often many times more valuable in this life (and other lives that you may or may not live in the future).

Sheila and Kiri ate and purchased their way toward the door

and into the twilight. They returned to the Marriott and brushed their teeth with their new toothbrushes. They bathed and put on new nightgowns and discussed what they might have for breakfast. "Why not choose everything?" suggested Kiri. "In this way, no delicious thing shall escape our taste of it."

"We wouldn't want that," said Sheila. She circled the Deluxe menu on the room service card and showed Kiri how to hang it on the brass doorknob.

The next morning two Deluxes were wheeled to the door by a smiling red-cheeked man who wore a short red jacket and asked where they wished to have the table placed. There were sugar-dusted rolls and half-moon omelettes and French toast on silver trays, as before. There was bacon that was neither too limp nor too crisp. There was sweet honeyed ham dressed with yellow arcs of pineapple. Piled in a small pyramid atop a crystal compote dish were plums, pears, apples, oranges, and bananas, each colored as if by an artist, without a bruise or scratch to mar their skins. To the side were chocolates wrapped in gold. At the middle of the table that stood just where they wanted it to stand, there was a fresh and perfect rosebud, just as there had been the day before and as there would be for days after.

Everything beautiful, everything clean, everything delicious, everything at hand, every everything and more everything, thought Kiri as she unrolled a croissant. Kiri did not feel sated by these wonderful everythings. What more might be had? she wondered. She did not want to discover herself to be a fool who was blind to the obvious. As she nibbled a slice of bacon, she remembered the uniformed government officer who had spoken to her on the day she entered the United States of America. He had given her one very plain order: Enjoy. And she had sworn to follow his order. Oaths being bonds, it was her duty, and finally she might be able to perform it. But how? For if, in only two days of freedom, there was this much everything to

be enjoyed, then, obviously, what she had considered everything was actually not, and what she considered enjoying now
might prove to be something far less. Clearly there had to be
more than the everything so far, but what? What endless, ever
delighting more and more? Kiri reasoned that it was her duty
to know, for how else might she fully discharge her obligation
to enjoy?

That afternoon, Sheila and Kiri went swimming in a vast
green pool edged with rocks, surrounded by palm trees and
vivid red hibiscus. The temperature of the air and the water
inside the Marriott's tropical atrium was so precisely matched
to the human body that it did not feel like any water or air
either woman had ever been in. On their skin, they felt only
the slightest tickle as they lost the pain and weight of their
bodies to a mysterious buoying caress. When they turned onto
their backs they could see the gray winter sky. That afternoon,
and for five more afternoons after that, they returned to weight-
lessness and watched the dancing snow fall lightly on the glass
roof and melt away without touching them.

Lincoln Leaves the Marriott

To put it succinctly, Sheila felt like a latter-day Abraham Lincoln. True, she had found and freed only one slave— BUT SHE HAD FREED A SLAVE. Clearly, she had done good. Having done good, such an absolute, indisputable good, and so soon after her resolution to change her life, Miss Sheila Jericault came to the conclusion that her redemption was more or less in the bag. Easy. I seem to recall seeing the word *easy* drift through her thoughts. Well. Ease, not to mention redemption, is, as that mischievous Albert Einstein used to say, relative. And it is also, often, entirely beside the point. Was creating your known universe, the galaxies of stars and planets, the many moving gases, fullness and voids, gravity and its opposite, the light, heat, cold, water, and what you know as matter as it appears in its living and unliving forms *easy*?

But leaving the universal value of ease to the side, it meant something to Sheila as she sat in her armchair at the Marriott, eating smoked salmon with capers and onions on elegant triangles of toast and feeling like Abraham Lincoln. She had done good, she felt like a better person, and that made her happy.

Presto. The "what" in her question "Now what?" had been tidily answered in a satisfying way, and she could go on from this moment with a well-stuffed, comfortable sense of what one might call completion. Easy.

But Sheila's "what" was beginning, not ending, and ease had nothing to do with it. Having told you that, I will further add that you must not think for a moment that it would have required any effort on my part to dissolve her bold presumptions. Had I been ignoring Miss Sheila Jericault entirely, or had I, for instance, come upon a more compelling diversion and turned my attention away, leaving her to fend on her own, her hubris still would have dissolved. Of necessity. You might say: Easily. Even if her soul, Grace, and various other matters that might or might not be of great import to your kind had not been at stake. Humility is rarely something humans need be taught by their gods. Voluntarily or involuntarily, they usually teach themselves. Or not. And we watch and we care or we don't do either. Depending.

So: Kiri chose a bagel and spread a chive-flecked layer of cream cheese across its toasted surface. She tasted her finger and added a thinly sliced tomato. While she contemplated what to put on next, she stirred a teaspoon of honey into her milky Earl Grey. Sheila was very quiet this morning and Kiri wanted to know why. She would not, by her nature, have been disposed to ask, so she waited, nibbling and sipping.

Finally, Sheila said, "Too bad we can't stay here forever." And then she sighed until she ran out of air.

Kiri waited for more. Why could we not stay here forever? she wondered silently.

As if in answer, Sheila said, "We gotta face reality sometime."

Now Kiri was entirely confounded. Was this not reality? It most certainly was. To dream this magnificent time of enjoying in such detail so soon after her enslavement would have been impossible, beyond her imagination's powers. And her eyes could see. Her lovely things were before her. She wore new panties and a new brassiere. Were they not real? By any standard she might apply, their reality was more than apparent.

Sheila sighed again. Abraham Lincoln had not been paying two hundred eighty dollars a night, plus room service, extras, and tips. Not to mention the shopping. She would deal with that later. Not that she had regrets. No regrets at all. It was just . . . "Checkout's eleven. We have time to maybe take a last swim," said Sheila. "If we pack up right after breakfast."

Now Kiri sighed. But her sadness passed with the exhalation of her breath. If there had been such wonderfulness at the Marriott, what awaited her beyond? What more? It would be necessary to leave the Marriott to discover this, she reasoned, and so smiled and said, "Everything will be very very very fine."

Sheila packed the fruit in the compote dish and made two sandwiches, which she wrapped inside the white cotton Marriott napkins. "For the road," she explained as she poured herself another glass of fresh-squeezed orange juice and traveled into a pleasant thought about the sweet taste that filled her mouth and washed away the taste of fish and onion.

With Kiri beside her, Sheila drove slowly through the sleet. She looked past the icy arrows that bounced off the windshield, saying nothing, thinking about how she and Kiri might become a team of sorts, become the best of friends, start new lives together, both of them.

It did not occur to Kiri to ask where Sheila was taking her.

Sheila did not know of a way to tell her.

They listened to the radio. Sometimes they sang. Sometimes they traveled away from each other, the car and the road, each in her own thoughts.

In just over three hours, too soon, Sheila signaled and turned onto Currier Street. Kiri gasped. "Don't worry," Sheila said quickly. "But get down." Kiri did not have to be told. At the sight of the Babahanis' hedges, Kiri felt her shoulders shrink into a hunch. She forgot to breathe. As quickly as her freedom had lifted her high, she was fallen, a slave again, a slave awaiting punishment for having dared to fancy herself free. A great punishment. A deserved punishment. A blow. A beating. Worse. Annihilation. Kiri's terror was like a shriek so loud it could not be heard, only felt as a killing presence in the ears, and Sheila felt it as surely as if it were her own. "You are safe with me," she said firmly. Make me not a liar, she prayed. Abraham Lincoln had left the Marriott. Now what? she asked herself as she placed a reassuring hand on Kiri's bowed head.

If she had known of the Mrs.' fury at Kiri's escape, of the deportation and subsequent execution she had threatened, Sheila might have made other plans. But she did not know of this or of the healing presence of yet another indentured girl, obedient and scared, who had rapidly taken Kiri's place. It was Kiri's worthlessness in the eyes of the Babahanis that saved her from immediate pursuit and prosecution. It was too much bother, too humiliating, to deploy the law to exercise their wrath, though it would have been dangerous to test their decision. It was the Mr. who said, "Why distress yourself, my beloved? It spoils your beauty," reminding his wife that it was only a servant, who would probably starve or find herself in prison, as well she deserved. The Mrs. was comforted, but not entirely. She felt robbed and would have liked to whip the little nothing for her cheek. Nonetheless, she deferred to her husband, and together they wished her ill, lied to their children about her absence, and moved on to more important matters. By the time Sheila and Kiri returned to Currier Street, Kiri was more or less safe, as long as she remained unseen and out of mind.

"Don't worry," said Sheila. "You're with me." Kiri released her fear, shoved it away. How could she insult Sheila with distrust? Sheila who had given her freedom. Sheila who carried a small golden card that made it possible to have in your hands everything you might desire. How could she doubt her?

Sheila pulled deep into the Onthwaites' driveway so that her car could not be seen from the road. Little balls of ice slapped Kiri's face as the two women gathered their packages and hobbled behind the big house to a small door. Sheila unlocked the door. Kiri looked up the narrow staircase, lit only at the landings. It was papered with morning-glory vines climbing white trellises, and the carpet was the color of late summer grass, but the attempt at cheer was unconvincing. The dim light reminded her of the Babahanis' servant quarters in Kuwait. Kiri fought with her own suspicion. Perhaps this was a trick. Or a test. If it was a test, she must prove her worthiness.

Sheila grimaced as she climbed. She could no longer ignore the weight of all their purchases. She stopped at the second landing, panting. She pressed her arms against her middle to somehow contain the pulling pain in her belly. "Man, I overdid it," she whispered, closing her eyes as she slid her back down the wall and rested against the painted vines until her body could endure another twelve steps.

Kiri asked no questions. Not knowing what to make of Sheila's discomfort, she stared at a spot near the wheezing radiator; she noticed that where the metal had rusted, the wallpaper had also grown tired and curled to show the yellowed paste on the underside. Kiri thought of the long carrot ringlets that dressed their salads at the Marriott. Who would have thought a root from the ground could be made to take such a charming shape? Looking up the last flight, Kiri considered the possibility that new splendor hid behind the door like a clever tiger choosing to crouch where he was least expected. There had been endless wonderful surprises. And now?

There was no wonder behind this door. Kiri could barely disguise her alarm and disappointment. A sagging couch, an aged and dusty television, an unmade bed with a raggedy robe strewn over it, a simple table with a bowl of withered grapes on top. This was not at all, even slightly, right. Though the room was not nearly as bad as the quarters she had inhabited, it was altogether without splendor, except perhaps for the size of the television and the lacy curtains. This was not what she expected from her Sheila, not after the Marriott, not at all, and certainly not what she expected of her freedom. "Very very nice," Kiri lied, walking round and round the modest room in which Sheila lived, looking for some sign of wickedness or a trap, nodding her head like a dashboard ornament. "Yes yes yes yes yes." She did not understand. How could someone with the golden card live in quarters little better than a paid servant's? Kiri giggled in fear.

"It's modest, but it's home," said Sheila, falling onto the couch and carefully lifting her legs up to the armrest. She closed her eyes again, and within minutes she was overcome by her own exhaustion. Kiri sat at the kitchen table watching Sheila Jericault's chest flutter up and down. She stared at the television, wishing to turn it on for company. She considered searching for the remote, but her thoughts brought her to her mother. Her mother did not know that her own daughter had been abundantly favored by destiny and captured into freedom, but she also did not know that Kiri had ever known the sorrows of slavery. And now, no matter what her mother knew, she, Kiri Srinvasar, had the fortune of one thousand dollars, cash gathered in one day. How much more could she gather? Endless more. Soon she would be able to send for her mother, her sisters. Then they would return to the Marriott and make it their home if by that time Kiri had not located an even greater magnificence. They would all have lovely golden cards imprinted with opalescent birds that seemed to fly even as they stayed in place. She would take them to the Marriott, and to the Nutmeg Country Mall. She would take them to Dallas and Hollywood and New York, New York, and servants with red jackets would bring their food. They would win lotteries and valuable prizes. And so, they would need nothing they did not want to need. As often as it pleased them, every day or twice a day, once a week or once a month, they would float on their backs in the still, warm water, never fearing the weather or the ticpolonga viper and its poisons. Everything would actually and always be very very very enjoyably fine indeed. There would be no old couches with green flowers and frayed arms in her paradise. Kiri was sure of that. No matter what there was before her now, there would be nothing but beautiful and endless more beautiful when the proper time came. That was Kiri's oath to herself. On Buddha's tooth, she swore it.

More Freedom

S lave taking is a human business and thus messy on the best of days. Slave having and freeing are fairly straight-forward, assuming a minimum of resistance. But the business of *being* free—what to do with your earthbound free-dom and what it means and requires and all that, while still wrapped tight in mortal coils—is a task, an art, from my point of view, that humankind rarely masters. There are so many questions. So many. And so many answers. None exact. And, as you are given to say, God knows the human passion for exactitude. Given all I have seen when I care to look, I was hardly surprised when after three or four days in Sheila's attic dormer, both Miss Sheila Jericault and Miss Kiri Srinvasar found themselves distinctly uncomfortable. And the small space was the least of it.

Sheila slept in her bed. Kiri slept on the couch Sheila's mother had recently occupied. They'd gotten the hang of sleep-ing in the same room at the Marriott and neither snored, at least not to a disturbing extent. So the sleeping part was basi-cally fine, dreams aside.

It was the matter of being awake that seemed to be the problem, being awake and alive with a future yet to be determined. And this might be said to have something to do with dreams not aside.

Sheila had neither clearly thought nor clearly dreamed about the aftermath of her Great Gesture. Without examining the probability, Sheila vaguely assumed something like this: that freedom had its own momentum and that somehow the freed Kiri Srinvasar would fly up and off somewhere, wings mended, brilliant in her new plumage, as Sheila waved from below, squinting with satisfaction into the whiteness of the warming sun. But Kiri preferred to sit in front of the television, holding the remote in her left hand, pressing buttons with her thumb.

From Kiri's point of view, there was nought else to be done because whatever the moment was that she was waiting for had clearly not come, or, more exactly, Sheila had not produced it.

Sheila did not know this feat was expected of her, part of the freedom deal. She shopped. She cooked. She rested and she cleaned. She loaded their laundry load after load after endless more loads into the miniature stacked washer-dryer, and through it all she listened not to the story of Kiri's life or tales from her homeland, as she might have wished to do, but to the perpetual chirruping of QMN spokesmodels alternately seducing and threatening viewers to buy now buy now call now right now, or lose this one-time-only opportunity. Sheila found herself sitting on the toilet long after she'd made use of it, long after she'd thumbed through this or that catalog or reread this or that short article. On the toilet seat, she sought a refuge from the invocations on the Quality Merchandise Network, but when the selling was dulled, she heard herself, and what her self had to say did not please her, so she sat, bare-bottomed on the hard plastic, alternately scolding and defending herself for and against her growing irritation. Even the very fact of feeling irritated made her irritable. This was hardly how she'd supposed things were supposed to be.

One day Sheila sat so long that when she rose, her knees ached and she became slightly dizzy. The toilet seat had imprinted a red oval on her bottom. And she thought: That's enough.

"Kiri?" she began carefully.

"Mmmm . . ." Kiri murmured. Sheila could not tell whether she'd actually been heard. Kiri's eyes were on the television. She was examining a blue sapphire ring with matching necklace, earrings, and bracelet, listening closely to the details about comparable prices elsewhere as enumerated by the spokesmodel on the Quality Merchandise Network. "So why pay more for less?" asked the spokesmodel in a reasonable tone.

"Why?" asked Kiri.

"Why what?" asked Sheila.

"Pay more for less when it is possible for one to pay less for more."

"Oh. Kiri?" Sheila began again. "Have you, uh, given any thought to . . . the, um, your . . . future?"

"Ah, yes. Certainly certainly," Kiri responded. She turned her attention to the next product on-air.

Perhaps, thought Sheila, she had not asked the question correctly. She waited for the spokesmodel to finish describing the many ways in which a watch with interchangeable watchbands and rims could be both practical and glamorous. "A whole wardrobe of watches in one!"

"Mmm . . ." said Kiri, considering this. "Do you not think such a watch would be quite a boring lot of bother in the end?"

"Mmm . . ." Sheila answered. She forced herself to press ahead. "Have you done any thinking about, like, what you might, like, want to do about, um, finding . . . something . . ." She hesitated, not wanting to be insensitive to Kiri's recent past. "You know, uh, something to . . . do?"

"I thank you for the very kind asking, but I assure you most certainly that you must not worry. I am not in the least thinking of that at all."

Sheila was stunned. She could think of no way to reopen the conversation. She resisted the urge to return to the bathroom. Staring out the window at the Babahanis' house, she wondered if the slave she freed would remain planted on her couch in her living room eating and watching game shows and coveting QMN bracelets and earrings forever. Torture. Damnation. That will teach me, she thought, reflecting on the consequences of her Good Deed. And then, instantly, she rebuked herself, for had she not done it, what? Kiri would still be a slave. And so it went in Sheila's mind, back and forth like fraying bow-strings, back and forth, a cacophonous screech against the saccharine symphony of spokesmodels, back and forth, resent-ment and rebuke, and the eternal question: Now what?

It had at last occurred to Sheila that her freed slave was more than a concept or a deed, more than an excuse to feel won-derful, then lousy, more, even, than an overwhelming and un-intended responsibility. She was a person, and as a person, Sheila, in spite of her deep wish to do otherwise, found her increasingly difficult to like. She was pleasant enough— Whenever was she not pleasant? She was almost annoyingly pleasant—but offered little of herself. Kiri was like a narrow-necked copper lamp, buried so long, jammed shut so tight, that it would not or could not reveal its contents. What was inside her? Vile stinking mold or rare perfumed Oriental oils? Was she filled with ancient meaningless dust or unannounced, inacces-sible powers? What? What was unrevealed? Was her hiding pur-poseful or unintended? Sheila would have taken any answer, as long as it was an answer, preferably true. She felt the need to have at least some knowledge of the woman whose life was now much more a part of her own than she had ever intended, and so Kiri's smiling, agreeable, impenetrability felt like a cruel re-fusal. Sheila had begun to feel that if indeed they were bound together forever, at the end of forever, whenever that was, they would still be strangers. Why was Kiri not an inspirational freed slave—worthy of an uplifting novel or a four-part miniseries on television—noble, rich with virtue, open of heart, generous, warm, wise? Just for instance. Why did she have to be so completely annoying? Sheila felt cheated. Sheila felt hurt. Sheila felt like a reprehensible idiot for feeling the way she felt and her tall-hatted Abraham Lincoln sense of having done right for right's sake was mightily tattered. But at least Sheila felt.

To get away from her own mind, she took herself downstairs to the mailbox. Clouds gamboled across the winter sky, pushed by a strong, high wind that she did not feel. On the ground the air was still. It calmed her. And so, calmly, she reached into the mailbox and drew out two fat bills, one slim letter, and a postcard.

She could tell the contents of the bills by their heft, so she chose not to open them. The postcard was of two young lovers, clothed roughly in the fashion of Adam and Eve, walking hand in hand on the sand toward a Floridian sunset. It announced her mother's elopement with Jerry with no further details. The letter was from the Onthwaites.

"Big news," said Sheila as she opened the door.

"Mmm!" said Kiri, her inflection indicating specific interest in Sheila's remark, though her eyes remained trained on a spokesmodel's turning wrist as it displayed the 18-karat gold bracelet laden with jewel-studded holiday charms that was now on offer. "A fine purchase?"

"My mother just remarried, and we have to move," Sheila blurted as she dropped herself onto the couch and fixed her own eyes on the ruby-nosed reindeer dancing across the screen.

"Ah," said Kiri. "It would certainly be a difficulty to fit two others to live in this close-together place, though, of course, it could certainly be a thing one could possibly do." Kiri pretended to think, though she already knew exactly what she thought. "Perhaps returning to the Marriott now would be very wise and best. It is filled with rooms."

Sheila laughed, though she suspected Kiri was not joking. Once again, she scolded herself. She had only herself to blame if Kiri thought she was living with a human horn of plenty. "I would never in a million years . . ." She hadn't the energy to untangle Kiri's thoughts. "Never mind."

Together they sat regarding the televised twinkling of a tiny sapphire-eyed Santa in his red cloisonné suit, the eight-tipped golden snowflake, and so on. Sheila was, for once, glad of the merry distraction. Finally, she rose and took a can of tomato soup from the cupboard. She emptied the contents into a pot and stirred in a cup of skim milk. She stood over the stove, watching the orange bubbles slowly form and slowly pop, thinking of stupid dinosaurs stumbling into voracious tar pits and being sucked in, suffocated. She inhaled the sweet steam as she pictured the black and sticky bones that had fascinated her as a child.

Then Kiri conspicuously cleared her throat. "I would very much be most grateful if you would consent so very very kindly to assist in the writing of a letter to my family and my mother at home."

Sheila felt as though her unsaid prayers had suddenly been heard and answered. At last, a sign of trust, an opening through which to pass. "I'd be delighted!" She turned down the flame under the soup.

"Perhaps you are wondering why it is not I who will be writing this letter myself?"

Sheila had not wondered. "Yes. I was."

"Ah . . ."

"Why?"

"Certainly I have not been writing words in so very long a time that I am most fearing my mother and sisters will see that the hand with which their Kiri writes is no longer strong but feeble and poor, and thus they will become most unnecessarily terribly worried of an illness when I am truly very very fine. I had a pretty writing once," she explained. "Now it is better in another hand, and the English writing will please them in a letter from the United States and Connecticut."

"Yes," Sheila agreed. "They'll be so happy. I'm sure of it. In any hand I'm sure they'd just be happy, but if you want me to, sure, yes. I'm honored to help."

Kiri turned off the television. Sheila rooted through her desk for a sheet of stationery that could lend beauty to a letter as important as this was to be, but there were only legal pads to be found. "I'm sorry, this will have to do," she said, selecting a smallish pad, the brightest and smoothest of the lot.

Kiri took a wooden spoon and gave the thick soup a gentle turn. "My dearest mother," she began. "I am writing now by way of the very kind penmanship of a friend, for I have only slightly sprained my writing hand and must rest it for some days and then it will be perfectly fine and as better as new. I have you always in my heart and now I write to you with wishes that you are very very well and all the others and Laxmi, Shankari, Miriama, and Jasi are all very well with you in the home or at the home of their husbands if they are married now because it is so long I have had news from you. It is so long that it could be Laxmi has given grandchildren to you and even so with Shankari.

"I have you eternally in my heart and I am wishing we will be together in the soonest time. This letter is not coming to you from Kuwait City where you expect because now I am in America and Connecticut and it is very beautiful here with white snow.

"There are many ways to find money. Even in very recent days I have had splendid fortune come to me directly and I am very very well with it. It is sorrowfully sad that I must also announce to you of the sudden death that my dear employer Mrs.

Babahani suffered in a fever that came on her. So it is that her husband will take the children back with him to Kuwait and they are very sad to bid farewell to me. The children weep that they shall never find another like your own and faithful daughter Kiri, who has certainly been so terribly good to them as if they were my own, and so the Mr. has begged for me to stay but I must wisely remain with my destiny in America these days."

In her astonishment at Kiri's dictation, Sheila stopped writing. Kiri placed one hand gracefully atop the other and waited for Sheila to pick up her pen before she continued without the slightest acknowledgment that Sheila knew these words were not the truth.

"He has been most extremely kind and thus has made a great payment to me of much money and so do not worry at all about the money to you. I am sending here five hundred of American dollars with this letter and there will be much more after this in the right time. America is a very lucky place and I am wishing to bring you to me here and will soon be fulfilled with joy when we are all together again. You must certainly meet my extremely good chum Sheila, who has been so very kind I shall never repay." Kiri smiled. "I will write again with news of more great happiness. I am sending again the most great quantities of love to you and this five hundred dollars as well."

"That it?" asked Sheila. "You want to send this?"

"Yes yes. Thank you for the very kind writing. I will be very happy if you will post it straightaway and I will have a reply I hope soon."

Kiri poured them both a cup of soup, but Sheila no longer wanted to drink it. Shiela tore the page she had written from the pad and passed it to Kiri. Kiri signed her name at the bottom in a swirling script unlike any Sheila had ever seen. She folded the yellow page in thirds.

"Yellow is one of my favorite colors, although the topaz is a lesser gem," said Kiri. "I have need of a yellow diamond in this freedom," she said as she cradled and caressed the television remote control in her hand as if it were covered in the softest velvet. Passing her thumb over the ON button, she turned her eyes expectantly to the television set as the picture appeared, a dot and then whole, upon the screen.

With the Letter in Her Hand

With the letter in her hand, Sheila set forth. Though the act of posting Kiri's lying missive might have been a simple matter of dropping the same into one of those ubiquitous blue metal boxes, naturally—for why else would I be interested?—it was not. Though lying had been one of the more creative parts of her job, Sheila had not considered herself a liar. Sometimes she saw her facile interpretations or reinterpretations of truth as a matter of practicing sculptural technique, as in "recasting the issues." Sometimes, the facts just needed blurring with a gyroscopic distraction provided by a quick verbal twist of her deft verbal wrist. This she would call "spin." Sometimes lies—if you define lies as untruths, which seems, from my point of view, to be the most utilitarian way to put it (leaving aside, from your point of view, the possible undefinability of truth, that most volatile of earthly gases, an element that, to the human kind, seems both the most valued and the most dispensable commodity)—were called simplification, elaboration, even clarification.

But Kiri's letter, though it certainly recast the issues, spun, simplified, elaborated, and thus in a false way, clarified, struck Sheila as shameless mendacity.

The weight of the letter on Sheila's newborn conscience was not merely a figure of speech. The envelope felt heavy to her, and seemed to grow heavier as she slid it in her purse. Pressing her foot to the gas, she felt an odd mechanical hesitation and thought, The car does not want to carry this letter. She pressed harder, overriding the car's resistance. She had written the letter in her hand, but the lies were not her lies, she reasoned. It was up to Kiri to say what she wanted, but why would she say what she said? Why was the story she chose better than the truth? "It's probably cultural," Sheila said out loud as she pulled into the parking lot, but that did not soothe her.

At the post office a man held the door. "I'm not going to hold it all day, dear," he said, smiling at Sheila's distracted shuffle. Sheila smiled back, but speed was beyond her. She was heavy with the letter and heavy with her thoughts and the handle of her purse pressed a red furrow into her arm.

As she waited in what seemed to be the longest line in which she had ever waited, she considered the money. Kiri was generous. She'd sent half of all she had. And that, certainly, was good. There was five hundred dollars, American cash, wrapped tightly in three layers of yellow legal paper inside the envelope. Money for Kiri's family, and surely a signficant amount. Kiri sent love, money, and preposterous lies. She must have her reasons, Sheila thought, and wondered if she ought to change the money, open the envelope and substitute an international money order to ensure that the five hundred dollars, the good part, arrived. But she decided against that idea. The letter was sealed. Let it stay sealed, she thought. The clerk weighed the envelope that, to him, seemed as light as any other letter. "It's right on the border," he said. "A dollar. Or to be on the safe side, a buck forty." Sheila chose the safe side and slid a dollar and four dimes across the counter.

Even with the letter gone, Sheila was not free of it nor was she free of Kiri, the freed Kiri to whom Sheila was feeling captive. And rightly so. She was bound to Kiri in more ways than she could know. She was bound by destiny. But at that moment, it seemed to her that the burning chafe of the tightening bind could be neatly relieved with a snip of sharp scissors. All I have to do, she thought, all I have to do, is . . . is . . . is . . . She dared to say it to herself: Get rid of her.

She walked to the newsstand and picked through the newspapers, sheepishly, as if she were perusing pornography in the wrong place at the wrong time. Finally, she bought every paper published in Connecticut, and carried her loot to the Windmill Diner. She ordered roast chicken because it would take time, and as she waited, she extracted and examined the classified ads in each edition. There was work that Kiri might do, plenty of it. Full-time, part-time, live-in, live-out, and as she circled the notices that looked the most promising, Sheila breathed in the diner air, breathed it deeply, as if it were fresh and cool. She smelled apples and cinnamon. She raised a hand and ordered pie to come before her chicken. The pie was sweet, with bits of walnuts and raisins in it so that each mouthful tasted very slightly different from the one before. It was as she finished eating this marvel of a pie and the main course was brought that a problem she had put aside demanded her attention. She had freed a slave. And the slave she had freed had no passport. No passport, no papers. A problem. But, Sheila reminded herself as she pressed her fork into her mashed potatoes, she was a strategist. She watched the gravy flow like lava through the white mound and onto her chicken and pressed again. She decided to call whoever it was that needed calling and straighten out the whole matter. Fast. This decision pleased her, and to the side of her meal, on top of the papers, she placed a napkin. On the napkin, she began a list. Sheila wrote, 1. 2. 3. And having made this list, she enjoyed its tonic effect and savored her chicken though it was underseasoned and a bit dry.

When she finished her meal, she drove to Grimaldi Drug Store, where they had a relatively private bank of telephone booths at the rear of the building. Now, as those of you who are phone-owning adulterers know, the sudden disposition toward the use of hidden phone booths is a story that tells itself.

Feeling disloyal, and at the same time vainly assuring herself that there was no reason, no point, no need, no need whatsoever, for her own discomfort, she placed a credit card call to the United States Immigration and Naturalization Service in Washington, D.C. She was confident. She knew how to deal with government types. What she did not know was immigration law, and what she learned was this: that Kiri, with her A-3 visa, had none of what the Action Answer specialist called "status." Having left the Babahanis, no matter what the reason, she was now subject to arrest and deportation if she was found. She was what the AAS called an "illegal." Meanwhile, her captors, being diplomats, were probably beyond prosecution. There was no use creating a scandal. Sheila asked what might happen if this statusless illegal (for having heard this much she was not about to name names) was offered a new and proper job, say, a job she found in the classifieds. The answer stirred the food in her stomach and put an end to Sheila's first hopes for her own liberation. If Kiri was offered a new and proper job and thus requested a permit to stay, the prospective employer, Kiri, and therefore Sheila, would have to be prepared to wait from three to fifteen years to begin. Between the present and the undeterminable beginning, there was nothing, nothing legal, to be done.

"So how are people supposed to *live?*" wailed Sheila in desperation.

And the Action Answer Specialist answered, "That's not the government's problem."

Sheila returned the phone to its cradle and wept, but not for long. She slid onto the cushioned seat of her car and started the motor. The car rumbled. An Englishman explained the second act of *Tosca*. Sheila listened and Sheila sat. For some reason, instead of driving away, she opened her purse and dumped it on the seat beside her. She did what women do. She picked through the feminine debris, dusting off the Kleenex pack, returning aspirin and lipstick to her cosmetic case and zipping the zipper. She removed her money from her wallet and ordered the one-, five-, ten-, and twenty-dollar bills. She counted her quarters and put the dimes, nickels, and pennies in the empty ashtray, and wistfully wished for the easy old days when the ashtray was filled with ashes. Every other thing being tidied, she sorted through the miscellaneous papers feathering the bottom of her bag. Along with the LifeSaver wrappers, the gasoline receipts, and the cash register tape, there was Bob Wickett's telephone number written on the back of a worn receipt for services she had not been rendered. Bob Wickett. She stared at the numbers and considered the man. Poor Bob Wickett, she thought. He was alone with a kid and no help. And the poor kid with no mama. A kid ought to have a mama. Sheila thought of her mommy sadly. A mama ought to want to be a mama. Wickett ought to have a loving wife who loved his kid. If not a wife, somebody around the house. A feminine touch. Somebody to help. It was perfect. It was even a Good Deed. Sheila knew Bob Wickett was no friend of the law. Good all around. She left Tosca at the moment she agreed to satisfy Scarpia's lust for the sake of Cavaradossi's freedom, and dialed. When, for a second, third, and fourth time there was no answer at Bob's place, she carefully checked the number and dialed it again. When again there was no response, she cursed him for not having a telephone answering machine and returned to the car and poor heart-torn Tosca, who had by this time murdered Scarpia and placed candles and a cross by his corpse. Sheila reminded herself that patience was as valuable as persistence and sat through the opera's third act, through Tosca's hopeful reuinion with her beloved Cavaradossi, through Cavaradossi's mock mock execution, and then his death, Scarpia's betrayal from beyond the grave. Then she returned to the pay phone. As Tosca threw herself from a parapet, Sheila dialed Bob Wickett one more time, realizing as she did that she had memorized his number.

Why Bob Was Not Answering His Phone

Bob was, for the most part, an uncomplicated man and he was not answering his phone for an uncomplicated reason. He was not home. As meteors tossed themselves across the Milky Way, gorgeously unseeable by human eyes in the growing dusk, Bob Wickett drove up and down the aisles of a jammed parking lot. He and Boggy searched for a space to park the truck so they could do their errands. Bob was invoking my name, irritably demanding that I damn the many other mortals who wished to shop at the same twilight hour, but I was charmed by the sparkling firefly light of the clustered meteors adding their brief burst of white-tailed mayhem to the cosmos, and paid his requests not the slightest mind. He cursed and Boggy turned up the radio, knowing his father would not give up. They cruised past the phone banks at Grimaldi Drug only moments after Sheila had decided that Scarlett O'Hara was right and tomorrow *was* another day. They cruised past the bleak shell of what used to be the local Woolworth's. Then Boggy spotted brake lights across the lot. "Dad! Quick! Over by Videomaster!"

Bob hit the gas, maneuvering gracefully around pedestrians. He got the spot. He wouldn't have, but there was a toddler involved. Right in the middle of the desired space, the tiny child was having a magnificent tantrum with all the abandon of a pampered Titan. Bob waited while the mother loaded the thrashing, spitting, yowling babe into his car seat. "You were never like that," said Bob.

"Always a perfect angel, that's me," said Boggy. "So howsabout we pick up a video on the way home? A Clint. Two Clints."

"That's seven bucks right there."

"Yeah, but I'm such a good kid . . ."

Bob nudged his boy. "You get more mileage outa . . . I shoulda never told you that. I shoulda said you were hell on wheels."

"Too late."

"We'll see what I got left after the shopping."

Boggy settled for that.

Neither Bob nor Boggy had listened to the weather report, or they would have understood why Stop & Shop was the place to be. "Must've been everybody thought the same thought at the exact same time," said Boggy, who liked that idea and played with the what-if of it almost daily.

"Fuck that," said his dad as he loaded Life and Kix and Cheerios into his shopping cart. "Meet me at the frozen section. Pick out them kosher chicken nuggets. Not the other kind. They got dog feet and whatever. Jews don't allow that shit. If you want good meat, always buy with the Jews. Kosher. That's your guarantee," he instructed. He said it every time they went shopping.

"So you want the ones with the pig's dicks, right, Dad? And the duck tits?"

"Get outa here. Where'd you learn to talk? And pick yourself some veggie tables." He wanted ice cream, too, but he didn't have to tell the boy. No boy on this earth needed to be told about ice cream.

The checkout was forever, from Bob's point of view. It seemed to him that each and every woman in line had a dozen coupons, and all of those coupons were at the bottom of her purse, needing to be fished out one at a time. It seemed to him everyone in front of him and his boy had some damned item like celery root and the clerk had never seen it before, had no idea what it ought to cost, and had to hold up the whole works calling over the boss to solve the mystery. "I'm in no mood . . ." Bob muttered. His gun rubbed painfully against his ankle. He bent to adjust it in his boot. He would have taken the gun out, put it in his pocket like he usually did. But it wasn't the time or the place to do the most sensible thing, so he'd probably get a mean blister. "And I'm tired. I can't stand forever like I used to."

"How 'bout if I run ahead to get the videos?"

"How 'bout." Bob pulled a ten out of his wallet. "And get me some caramel corn. With the nuts, boy. Peanuts. Protein. So your sugar high ain't a total waste."

The boy was out the door. Maybe he'd heard about the nuts. Maybe not.

When Bob told the clerk he had no coupons, rather than check him through, take his cash, and be glad of it, the woman handed him a flyer and said, "Take a look. Better the money in your pocket." Made sense to Bob. He flipped through, ripping out the coupons that matched what he'd chosen. Got something off the Life and margarine, the ice cream and the laundry detergent. The cashier was almost as happy as he was, probably happier. "It feels great to save!" she warbled.

"It takes a woman," he said admiringly. As he pushed his cart out of the store into the lot, he thought about women. He didn't care about women as a bunch; who could care about a bunch of anything? But a woman, *one* woman, how would that be? Maybe a woman who liked to save. Or liked to fuck. Shit, Bob thought as he waited for the automatic door to shut so it could open again, from eight or nine years old every guy in this country was soaking up the sex, thinking it, selling it, buying it, renting it, reading about it and watching it on TV, phoning it up with the 900 toll calls, maybe even doing it, but it was doing it that got him a boy with no mother to raise him, and he had put sex mostly out of his mind. Most of the time. What about the cashier? he wondered. Nah. She'd saved him $2.71, almost the cost of renting a Clint for the boy, but sex didn't lead to no bargains. The way he saw it, you paid for what you got but you never got what you paid for. Sometimes more. Usually too much. Or a damned sight less. Never just the right amount, and anyhoo women were always . . . He dropped the thought. He saw something. The clouds were coming in blacker and the sky seemed lower, like it was getting down to have a look, getting too near, too close to him. The lot had cleared out. He noticed that, too. All those coupon fishers in line ahead of him had gone home with their discounts. And his truck. Was that someone climbing over the side panel? Was it? No doubt. Who the hell? Bob stopped. It wasn't Boggy. It didn't have Boggy's shape. "Shit," he whispered, crouching down beside the shopping cart to transfer the gun from his boot to his coat pocket. The shooter had come to finish the job. What did he want with the back of the truck? A bomb. Take his boy, too. Wipe them both off the earth. Where the hell was that boy? "Shit." Maybe it was a sneak job. Wait down in the back and then *blam!* right through the window, dead. "No way, you bastard," Bob growled.

He readied himself, moving to the rhythm of his furious heart; he pulled down the shopping cart's kiddie seat and lifted a grocery bag up on it to hide his face. He rolled the cart past the truck by three aisles and then up where he could get a look. The bastard was crouching. Bobbing. Bob moved up behind slowly, but not too slowly. The cart had a creak, and if it creaked too slow it'd call more attention than if it creaked like they all creaked. He pushed with one hand, his other drew the gun and placed it on a loaf of bread at the top of the brown bag that shielded his face. He needed a clear shot. Folks were coming and going. He had to get closer. Still didn't see Boggy, and that was okay. He was probably wandering the aisles of Videomaster. That boy could take a lifetime when it came to choosing even when he knew damn well what he wanted. Bob thanked me for the very trait he couldn't stand and asked that the boy linger longer, dwelling over photos of Clint Eastwood's stubbled face. He rolled up until he was half a dozen cars away. A gust of wind blew two feet of blond hair up out of the shooter's jacket. Was it a woman? Could it be Boggy's mother come back? Didn't matter who the hell, he thought. Maybe ten feet away, he could see that, yes, it was a goddamn woman. It was a woman. Against nature, a woman shooter. Bob dismissed nature. Nearly made his boy an orphan, woman or no woman, nature or no nature. He left the metal cart between a Jeep and a Toyota and crept low, just him and the gun. The woman was down low now. He'd get that unnatural bitch. Easy. Easy as she'd got him. But first she was going to look in his eyes. See who it was. See her victim. See her justice. Face-to-face, answer a few questions for Mr. Bob Wickett before she felt the lead.

She didn't hear him, the woman. Holding the gun just under his right eye, he centered himself between the back tires and began to rise up, his free hand steadying him as he peered over the back panel and said, "What the fuck you think you're trying to pull, ma'am?"

The bitch jumped and he nearly shot her then, but he held himself tight and calm. "Uh, uh, I, uh, the wind, uh . . ." She was crying.

It wasn't the tears that told him this wasn't the shooter. It was that sense he was counting on. The sense that would tell him what was true. That would make sure he knew for sure in his heart. Yes. Or no. The sense said no. Of course it wasn't a woman, wasn't this woman. "You ever heard of trespassing? I could have shot you," he said, and his voice shook thinking how close to could-have he came. "You look like a goddamn carjacker. I could have shot you stone dead and any court of law . . ." Bob sighed. "Now what the hell?"

The woman blinked her eyes over and over. He rested the gun and she relaxed slightly, not quite sure that she wasn't going to die at the hands of this raving crazy. "My scarf blew off into the back of your truck. And then . . . I found it, see?" She held the greasy fluttering silk up as proof. "But I got some grit in my eye and I took off my lens and the next thing I dropped it. Sorry. I'm really sorry. Really, please, I'm so sorry. I didn't mean to . . ."

"That's okay," said Bob, wanting to comfort her. "Wait here." The woman did not move. Bob rolled the shopping cart over to the truck. "I got a flashlight in my tool kit."

It was Boggy who finally found the lens. Leaning out the back window of the cab on his belly, he brought his arm level with the truck bed and shined the flashlight right to left, slow, low, and slightly sideways. In a couple of seconds, he saw the light nick a tiny curve near the spare, and that was that.

Bob saw no reason to tell the boy what had almost happened. No point. It hadn't. Had it? Bob was glad of that, and his boy had done good, so Bob and Boggy took themselves for fried chicken and coleslaw and the usual fries.

When they got home, the phone was ringing. It had stopped before they unlocked the door, so they just had to wonder. They didn't wonder long. They just put on the Clint and ate caramel corn.

The Clouds Deliver

The low clouds unloaded their cargo. They let go and go and go with even more snow than the hysterics had predicted, and those who had jammed the Stop & Shop lot were smug in the knowledge that they would not run out of milk or orange juice as they watched the yellow snowplows struggle to clear the roads. Boggy didn't have school, so he watched the Clint until in his mind he was Clint and he could say Clint's lines and squint Clint's squints. Bob let him. What the hell else was the boy supposed to do? He'd had him out shoveling, but there was no point. As soon as Boggy cleared a path, the snow would fill it up again. And Bob, though he had forms to fill, gave in to the weather, gave in and napped long hours in the morning and afternoon until, in a lazy way, he almost felt good. It was quiet. The phone rang but once, when sweet Mrs. March called to see if they were set with enough to eat.

The phone rang but once; however, Sheila dialed the Wickett's number obsessively, minute by minute, in her head. Her fingers were prevented from pressing the actual buttons on the telephone only by her confinement, for she, like all the other residents of Fallowfield and environs, was unable to leave the house and she could not make the call in front of Kiri—could not or would not. So she watched the snow fall and sat on the toilet and sat on the couch, she brooded, she obsessed, and she listened to Kiri comment in detail on that which the perky spokesmodels touted on the Quality Merchandise Network. Faster than the snow fell, Sheila's need to be rid of Kiri grew, stifling her breath, causing her to open a window and shove her head out. She sucked in the chill until it hurt her lungs, and exhaled a cloud of steam. Freedom, this particular freedom, felt like her ultimate need, the need of her life, and there was nothing she could do about it. Until the snow stopped. She, like Bob, sought refuge in sleep, but the good she had done was forgotten there, and her dreams were desperate and frantic.

By the colloquial measure of earthly time as calculated by you for centuries, the snow fell for a night, a day, another night, and another day, approximately forty-eight hours. By the experiential measure of earthly time, it fell too long for Bob. It fell too short for Boggy, who was beginning to fall in love with the amber Mexican girl who was in love with Clint, and thus did not want to have to return the video. The snow fell no time at all for Kiri, who had been only nominally aware of the weather, and it fell like a consuming shadow over Sheila's new life, which she was convinced would be ruined if she did not do something to decisively advance the cause of her emancipation from Kiri Srinvasar's freedom immediately. She studied the snowplows and the road beneath the window.

On the morning of the third day (which, as you recall, was the day the Bible endearingly mistook a naked singularity the likes of which your physicists can scarcely yet concieve for the simple fashioning of two great lights, the brighter to rule the day and the lesser the night) the roads appeared to be passable. Sheila set out on the icy roads under the cover of a woolly and lightless sky. There was no mishap. She made her way to the hidden phone booths behind Grimaldi Drug without so much as a skid. Her mind was so securely fixed on her plan that when she arrived and learned that phone service at the mall had been knocked out by the weather, rather than return home with the job undone, she waited with unusual patience, reading the newspaper until it was restored. When at last there was a dial tone, Sheila pressed Bob Wickett's phone number into the machine, exactly as she had done so many times the past two days in her imagination. Only this time the connection was made and the telephone rang and Bob answered, which made all the difference.

Only One Dream Comes True

All the while Sheila was plotting, Kiri had developed a few lesser dreams of her own. She had decided that it was necessary for her to mask her black tresses with yellow dye. All evidence presented by the television pointed to the advantage of this course. Kiri had determined that this dream had to be made real without delay by a return to the Marriott beauty salon, a return made possible by Sheila. As soon as a sign presented itself, she planned to ask Sheila to take her. Kiri had also decided that she must have her own plastic card. Her study of the QVM had shown her beyond doubt that there was nothing to be done in the way of having without such a card. And so she had resolved to ask Sheila about this as well. Two matters, then, needed her attention even as she waited for the greater enjoying to begin. It might be, Kiri reasoned, that the delay in the fullness of enjoying thus far had been the result of her inability to see the first steps on the path. Now she could see and needed only to set foot.

Thus, it seemed quite in the nature of things to expect when Sheila cleared her throat and suggested they turn off the television and take a little drive.

"Yes yes it would be lovely indeed," said Kiri eagerly. She switched off the television and, to Sheila's astonishment, gathered her clothes together. "I have awaited this time completely with my heart."

As you know and I know and Sheila soon learned, the time Kiri was awaiting was not the time that had arrived. Once they were in the car and under way, Sheila marshaled her courage and embarked upon a long and elaborate explanation of quite a simple fact: that Kiri was going elsewhere. She stammered, she stuttered, she cleared her throat, she said things three times round that might have been said once, and so on. As you are not a god and cannot be expected to have the vast patience we are truly or falsely credited with, I shall spare you the word-for-word. Sheila was neither cruel nor honest enough to tell the plain truth. She instead told a lot of related truths of varying purity and hoped they hung together. She explained, for instance, that for several reasons, all of which went unnamed but were made to sound unalterable and grave, it had become impossible for Sheila and Kiri to continue to live together for the time being. She explained that owing to the predicament presented by the absence of a passport and the presence of a violated A-3 visa, Kiri would have to live and work in a way that was invisible to the government of her new country, adding, "At least you won't have to deal with the IRS!" and forcing a jack-o'-lantern smile that owed much to her televised tormentors, the grinning spokesmodels.

"And the plastic card?" Kiri asked, for that was her second thought after her relief at being safe from that dreaded IRS, whose name seemed to cause horror whenever it was spoken. The rest had not yet settled in her mind.

"I don't know," Sheila lied. "Maybe."

Maybe wasn't yes, and Kiri was troubled by the space between the answer desired and that given. Kiri gaped at Sheila's overtoothy smile. It did not belong to her natural face. It was a strange smile on a strange face, and Kiri wondered if a cunning demon had contrived to enter her good friend whom she would never repay but upon whom she relied entirely. She said nothing as they passed the blotchy gray branches of the tired trees along Route 8A. Black and crust covered what was left of the great snowfall. The whiteness was a memory. Kiri contemplated Sheila's many explanations as a cloud of dismay gathered around her. Kiri wanted to cry out. Having brought her to this freedom, was Sheila not responsible? Was Kiri's duty to enjoy not bound to Sheila's duty to provide? How could she be released upon the world without so much as a golden card? This separation could not be true. It was not time. There was never to be such a time. It could not be so. But it was true and it was so, and the time appeared to be now. Finally, Kiri nodded and bobbed her head with exceptional vigor as if to say yes to the turn in her fate, which she might as well have done since no seemed an impossibility in a car moving fifty miles an hour.

Sheila turned onto 32 and found her way to Applewood. As her car leaped over bumps and swerved around potholes, Kiri studied the cattle along the roadside and found comfort in their obesity. She had never seen cows such as these, fat, enormous black-and-white beasts with invisible ribs. They roamed, clean and happy, jostling each other in a convivial way as they gathered, unbothered by cold, striped predators, or hunger, at a steaming trough. "Perhaps there is nothing to worry," she ventured.

"Nothing at all," Sheila assured her. "Everything is going to be just fine." They bumped for another few minutes. "We're looking for number 167."

"One sixty-seven," answered Kiri. "Ah!" She added the numbers. They made fourteen. Fourteen was written one-four. One and four equaled five. She wondered if five was a good number or if perhaps on the lottery she next played, one-six-seven-fourteen-five would be a lucky pick and bring the next great amount.

Suddenly Sheila doubted herself, or perhaps I ought to put that more precisely. It was impossible for Sheila to doubt her desire to rid herself of Kiri, but Sheila had room to allow that she wasn't entirely sure what she was doing, though it could be elaborately justified, especially by her, could actually be called right, even if it did have all the spots and stripes of a recognizable Good Deed.

For the sake of Sheila's seedling soul, which was reborn, but barely, still tenuously rooted by the merest opalescent thread, and from my point of view, deserved a chance to grow, I was pleased at her discomfort. She was not. She did not experience her straining conscience as a blessed sign of hope, for in her body it took the form of stabbing stomach cramps.

She spoke in part to comfort Kiri, in part to distract herself. "Now. Don't get alarmed when you see the place. It is . . . modest. Actually, a little rough. But that is exactly why I know you'll be so happy there. They need a woman's touch. And Bob's put a new TV in your room. Better than mine. And bigger, too. Of course, you don't have to . . ." Sheila stopped herself from finishing the sentence. "You'll love each other. A hundred twenty-five cash a week, no rent, and free board, so you'll have plenty to do what you want. And he only wants twenty, twenty-five hours, so that leaves you time to earn more, if you want to. Bob says, I mean if it works out, he told me he'll teach you to drive and he knows someone . . . Well, I'll let him surprise you. You'll love it, though. I'm sure you'll love it."

Kiri considered the money. "What if they do not pay?"

"This isn't Kuwait," Sheila answered. "Any problems, you come to me."

"If I am having any troubles?"

"Absolutely," said Sheila. "I am here if you need me."

I understood that to be a promise and noted it well, as did

Kiri. However, Sheila forgot her word as soon as it was spoken. She had seen 167 Applewood Road.

Boggy Wickett flicked his straight hair back from his eyes with a quick jerk of his head as Sheila's car scratched over the gravel to the door of the garage. He dug his hands deep into his front pockets and curled his shoulders forward. Then he threw them back and adopted what he thought might be a manly stance. He cleared his throat in case he was called upon to speak. His voice was changing. Who knew what sound might come out? He prayed it would be a manly sound and not some goatish warble. When Kiri pushed the car door open with her knee, Boggy saw what he immediately decided was the best thing he had ever seen: a miracle. Before him stood the amber señorita, Clint's woman. Almost. As close as a boy could hope to get, not being Clint and not being in a movie and this being his life, which was, from his point of view, about as far from amber señoritas as a life was likely to get. He could barely believe Kiri Srinvasar was three-dimensional. Based on the experience of his short lifetime, he knew that they, whoever they were, didn't have girls like this in Connecticut. At least not in his school. And not at the mall. He'd seen pictures of foreign women before and even kind of knew what they looked like all the way naked. His dad had a couple of crank-yanking magazines at the back of the top of the linen closet, but those girls were triple Ds, and probably half made out of plastic. The amber señorita who had just showed up was real. Boggy saw the curve of Kiri's breasts under her open parka and wondered if they'd be the brown silk color of her skin or maybe a lighter brown. Would they have the weighted softness of a cow teat? He'd touched lots of cow teats and none attached to girls. He wondered. He didn't know. On the spot, he prayed, truly prayed to his boyish god, that maybe by some unbelievable it's-about-fucking-time-something-good-happened-round-here miracle he would be lucky enough to find out.

"You must be Boggy," said Sheila.

"Um, yeah," said Boggy, who wasn't quite sure who he was right then.

"I know your dad from . . ." Sheila didn't know what she should say to the kid. Who knew what a kid that age ought to know? She started again. "I'm Sheila. And this is my friend Kiri, who is hopefully going to help out . . ."

"We could sure use you, um, around here. For help. We need a lotta help, um, definitely a lot." Kiri smiled, as did Sheila. Boggy bolted into the house. "Daaaad!" he shouted.

Bob was upstairs in his bedroom looking at himself in the mirror. Knowing Sheila was on her way, he'd showered and combed his hair back neat while it was still wet. He'd put on a clean pair of jeans and the patterned sweater Mrs. March had just knitted up for him this Christmas. He looked good. Like he was going somewhere. And looking at himself in the mirror, he was embarrassed at having got all fixed up. How come he was dolling himself? He had a mind to mess his hair and pull out the neck of the sweater so it looked stretched and old, make himself look regular, get comfortable. But the boy called him again.

"Daaaaaaaad! They're heeeeeeeere!"

Thinking of seeing Sheila again, Bob hadn't given much thought to the foreign girl. It seemed okay. Sheila Jericault had put it to him that it made total sense all round, so why not? As long as she didn't steal and she knew something about cooking, it might be fine enough. Maybe even better for the boy than he could do alone now with his strength less than it was and needing to pick up even more hours. He pushed his gun into his belt. He wasn't one for foreigners in general, but that wasn't why he did it. It was just habit. Like brushing your teeth. He stopped by the kitchen on his way into the living room. He grabbed the candy jar. "Boggy," he called out. "You offer these ladies a Coke or something? Coffee? We got orange juice with extra added calcium. What else?"

Bob felt a hard kick in his chest when he saw Sheila. She stood up and put out her hand. He wondered if she felt the same way he did, wanting to get away from the others, whisper the secrets alone between themselves, talk about IT, talk about surviving, if that's what they had done, and talk about life on the other side of death, how it made you be apart and passionate, sure and unsure, all at once.

As it happened, she did feel that way. Seeing Bob, she suddenly felt that he would understand how her spirit had shifted without consulting her mind, that he was the one person in the world she could tell. She was unable to look at his eyes, as if she would be discovered. She feared she might weep. So she looked away and said, "Hey, Bob, good to see you. How you been?" without waiting for an answer. "I'd like you to meet Kiri Srinvasar," she continued.

Bob nodded at the tiny dark woman who held Boggy so entranced and found himself uneasy about her good looks. "I remember you like Baby Ruths," he said, turning to Sheila, fishing the candy out of the jar and handing it to her.

"What a treat," she said.

"Want something?" He passed the jar to Kiri.

Kiri picked a Mounds bar. "Oh yes, thank you very much."

"You like Mounds? Cool. I love Mounds," said Boggy.

"Why'n't you show, uh, Kiri here where her room would be and the kitchen and where the usual stuff is?" said Bob.

Boggy jumped up. "So she's stayin'?"

Bob shrugged. "If she wants. Sure."

"Do you want to?" Boggy demanded, looking directly into Kiri's black eyes and seeing his own face reflected. "Say yes! Say yes!"

Kiri tilted her head and lowered her eyelids as if the desire in Boggy's eyes was of too great an intensity. She smiled at the boy's pleading. He wasn't like the Babahani boy. She knew he wanted something. She sensed he wanted to please her. Please *her*? Why? Another marvel in America. "Yes," she answered. She knew of no other answer that would do at present.

Boggy made a fist and held it in the air. "*Allll*right!" The others laughed, but he didn't care. "Come on," he said to Kiri. "Let me give ya a tour of the White House."

Bob slid into the chair Kiri left empty. Sheila watched his knee bounce and listened to his teeth crack the dry peanuts of the Baby Ruth as he bit it. "I think this'll all work out," she said.

"Yeah." Bob wished she'd start talking about what they both wanted to. He didn't know how. They sat and chewed candy instead.

When there was nothing left in her mouth, Sheila sighed. "It's weird, isn't it?"

Bob sighed back. "Too fuckin' weird for words."

"You okay?"

"I got unfinished business."

"I don't know if a gun's going to get you justice."

"I don't know anything anymore."

"It's like that."

"I hate it."

"It makes you feel . . ." Sheila didn't know how to finish the sentence.

"What it is," Bob said, "is that you know something big, something God didn't intend for you to know, like, until it was your time. And instead of it putting you ahead of the game, it just fuckin' changes the game you're in and you're living all right, but you ain't on the same damn playing field as before. I'll tell you that. That's what it fuckin' is."

"Sounds about right to me," said Sheila.

Bob rubbed his hand hard over his nose to rid himself of an itch, then he sniffed hard and said, "I saw on the TV some guy who said he technically died, like it's some fuckin' technicality and there's some whistle-blowing ref at the side. But anyways, then he says—I love this—he says he went down to hell and saw his punishment for being such a . . ." Bob laughed. "Now if I was him . . ."

"Did you believe it?"

"Fuck no. I think he's a money-making liar."

"I don't know."

"Gimme a break. What did you see?"

"Nothing. But maybe . . . I don't know. Maybe he believes that's exactly what he saw. What's he doing now? Did he turn good?"

"Can't say. Who's to say? But he was on TV. He got to whoop it up at the whatchacallit Netherlands Hotel out on Central Park and order up steak to his room and ride in a limo and maybe some girls, pardon my French. And be on TV. So . . ."

"Well, at least he got that."

"Not bad for a sneak preview of hell."

"Guess if he knows he's going . . ."

"Oh, but he said God or the Devil or someone told him personally you can turn it all around. Reverse your fate."

Sheila shrugged. "I'm trying."

Bob didn't think Sheila was agreeing with him in the way he wanted to be agreed with and he didn't want to feel bad about that, too, so he changed the subject. "Um, I had a word with Mrs. March about the manicuring job for your friend. She says that her friend says that it's okay. If your girl there is quiet and works strictly cash and tips. She's got a couple of Koreans do the same. She says her friend just won't ask and your friend—"

"Kiri."

"—Name doesn't matter. She might want to get another name, but any rate, Kiri just won't tell and nobody says nothing, so there should be no problem. Starts Monday."

Sheila nodded her head up and down, up and down, as if

she had briefly become Kiri. "Sounds good. Sounds great. Thanks."

"You want to tell her?"

Sheila did not want to tell Kiri. She felt the pain again. "Damn."

"You okay?"

"This damn thing . . ." Sheila started, but the damn thing was Kiri. Sheila worked. Bob Wickett worked. People just worked. That's what people did. So how come she felt lousy sending Kiri off to work? How come she felt she ought to be doing something more or something else? "No, you." She couldn't account for this feeling, not to herself and certainly not to anyone else. "It'll be good if it comes from you." She touched Bob's arm. "She's had a tough time, Kiri."

"Who ought to go to hell are those goddamn blanket heads kept her like a fucking slave."

"It would be nice if there was one to send them to."

"You tell me what the justice is, they walk off scot-free?"

"Diplomatic immunity. Different rules. Special parking."

"That's what we need," said Bob.

"Yup," said Sheila, reaching for the candy jar and another Baby Ruth. "That would solve a lot in a hurry."

Sheila's Own Freedom

I f you think I am about to tell you of a tear-splattered farewell, think again. I am uninterested and unmoved by the
moment of human partings in general, for whatever has
happened to bring them about has already happened, and
whatever will happen to illuminate them is yet undone.

However, I recognize that your perspective may be entirely
different. At minimum, you are likely to harbor an itchy curiosity. I will scratch it for you. But even having done so, I will
probably disappoint you, one way or another. If ever you feel
your chosen god has turned a deaf ear or worse, ask yourself
how acute your own hearing would be if, many times a minute
for many thousand years, one mortal or another were tugging
at you with vain expectations about what you were meant to
do to improve his or her lot. It is wearing and wearying, wearying and wearing, and mankind, who names us in all his languages and thinks of us as his, tends to assume, therefore, that
we are in his employ, as if we hadn't a universe or two to tend.
On account of human expectation, there is too much whining
altogether.

But as I have pledged, you shall have their good-bye as it happened. And you are warned I will brook no complaints if it isn't what you had in mind.

Kiri and Sheila parted with a quick hug and promises to see each other very very soon. Though Kiri was frightened and Sheila insincere, neither betrayed that truth to the other, and so there were smiles and waves on the driveway.

Now, let's away to more engaging matters.

My interest in Sheila, as you recall, was begat by an interest in Sheila's soul at a time when she had lost it. It was to the climate there that my attention turned, and for the moment, it was brilliant with wild, unfiltered sunshine that masked an unfelt chill. She rejoiced at her own found freedom many times more than she'd rejoiced at the saving of her barren life. She recognized the brisk gust of exuberance that caused her to fly even as she drove. She knew the feeling. She'd had it once not long before. Once when she made Kiri free. So, they were both free, she thought, and her Good Deed was done.

She sang and she took herself for oversweet sweet-and-sour chicken. She ate the pineapple bits with her fingers and ordered a second helping of tinned mandarin oranges; all sweetness tasted right to her. Sweet freedom, she thought, anticipating the silence that would greet her on her return home. As she climbed the stairs to her dormer flat, she heard only her feet. As she opened the door, there it was: the silence. And Sheila delighted in the noiselessly blank black face of the television set. "No spokesmodels!" she chortled, pulling her green mohair blanket around her shoulders and stretching out on the couch without consideration for anyone else because there was no one else. She spread out over both cushions, placing both throw pillows behind her head. She looked around the room. It was empty, but for her. She was alone, alone except for herself. "Alone," she said out loud. "Perfectly alone," she repeated. For several days her solitude—or if she was shopping and found herself in the company of other people, even the thought of her solitude—was enough to make her happy. Each time she thought only of herself, bought only for herself, she thought, Freedom.

But after the several days had passed, she remembered why it was she'd feared this very state. Unbidden the resting question rose and stretched. Now what? And unfortunately, from Sheila's point of view, the list of what there was now was unappealing. On it were the enormous questions, about Life and Meaning. But they did not stand alone like pillars to be passed through as she entered the temple of wisdom. They were crowded top and bottom with petty matters, nipping like maddening little dogs at her ankles, attaching themselves like streamers to her every thought. The Onthwaites wanted their attic back and Sheila had to move, which meant she had to *think* about moving and finding a place and where and how much and possibly why. The hospital wished to be paid for saving her life, and toward that end had sent her a partially itemized $29,875 bill, a bill and a price she resented in too many ways to consider. Discover, Visa, MasterCard, and Amex awaited full or partial repayment for their role in Kiri's spectacular introduction to abundance in America, and that was not all.

To her great perturbation and in spite of her will, she found herself missing the presence of the very person of whom she had yearned to be free, Miss Kiri Srinvasar. Impossible, she thought, but thinking did not make it so. Seeking distraction, she switched on the television and, seeing a citrine pendant set in sterling with matching earrings, switched it off, then on, then off again. What a terrible longing she felt. It took the form of hunger, and so she ate even more than she'd already been eating and still suffered from an emptiness. It took the form of fatigue, and so she lay prone, not quite able to do any one of the many things that awaited her attention. She stared out the window at the Babahani house, trying to discern movement behind the curtains, as if that would tell her something, but it told her nothing. The comings and goings were as they had been before Kiri's escape. Life appeared to be orderly. Nothing seemed to have changed. She wondered if she ought to simply telephone Kiri and say hello, but she resisted that impulse, from fear of where it might lead.

One doesn't know how long she might have stayed in this sad, weighted condition had she not heard unexpectedly from her friend and enemy, Mr. Hal Orinsek. I had nothing to do with that. The man had built his career on a certain preternatural sense of when to pounce.

"Darling!" he drawled into the phone. "I've missed you. The Onthwaites tell me you're moving. Without telling me? You bad thing. But I'm bad, too. I've been meaning to call ever since your unfortunate . . . How are you?"

"Fine. I'm great," lied Sheila, hating herself for being happy to hear from him. "Except . . ."

"Except what, pumpkin? Tell me what I can do."

"Oh . . ." Sheila sighed. "I'm just trying to sort things out."

"Poor kitten. Well, first off, where are you going?"

"I don't know."

Hal laughed. "And how much does 'I don't know' cost?"

"I don't know. Why?"

"Well, if you were looking, I might have a little something in the form of a job for you, a bit of consulting, you might say, if . . ."

"Then I'd say 'I don't know' costs a hell of a lot."

"Pride goeth, but we're none of us egoless in this business. And we both know you're a true talent. That's why it broke my heart when, uh . . ." The temperature in Hal's voice dropped several degrees as he recalled the recent Coxx debacle. If he was going to offer his wayward but cherished lamb redemption, which, as he saw it, was what he *was* doing, he wanted her to do some plaintive bleating first, to be, at very least, grateful, so he could tinker with her price. "Frankly, you, uh, did call Kip Coxx an asshole in his hour of need. Did you not?" he reminded her.

"Well, if I didn't, I should have."

Hal coughed in irritation. "Did you or did you not refuse to help your—I mean, our—client?"

"I was busy dying at the time, okay? The man totally nuked himself. No help from me."

"But my love." He decided to take her lack of repentance as folly brought on by youth and inexperience, and adopted a corrective tone. "The point is, you should have un-nuked him. Changed the perception. What do I always tell you? Perception is all. Credibility and perception and the perception of credibility. Surely, you weren't too dead to do a little better than suggest a fellow fuck himself? When he was down, Sheila. The man was down and you kicked him. Surely, you of all people know what a little compassion . . ."

Sheila laughed the way people laugh when their car spins over black ice and across the highway and there is nothing to be done but wait for the outcome. "You know what?"

"What?"

"There has got to be a god," said Sheila. "Because there's no other explanation. Not here on earth. Things are slow and God is bored, so he's having himself a little hoot at my expense. That has to be it. Because I can see no other reason in the goddamned universe why, on this particular goddamned day, I, of all people, ought to be having this particularly insane unasked-for conversation about how, if I understand you correctly, by basically practically bleeding to fucking death, I let down the side and disappointed Kip Coxx. Get this straight. I worked a fucking miracle on his behalf. That's what I did. But he needed more than I could do. A man has got to be bigger than his weenie, Hal. A little self-control . . . The minute I took my eyes

off that man, not because I wanted to, I had no choice—*ping!*—
out pops his twitchy little cock and *blammo,* it's over. The minute. He was going to win, damn it. There was no excuse."

"There's always an excuse."

"Say good-bye, Hal, because I don't want to be rude. I used
to love you and I'll feel like a shit if I hang up on you. I feel
lousy enough already."

She was being incorrigible, but Hal was not discouraged. He
had been the one who had not provided medical insurance, and
Sheila did not come from a wealthy family. Unless she'd been
amazingly thrifty, he figured she needed money. A lot of it.
"Don't hang up, honey."

"Then hold on." Sheila buried the phone between her knees
so that any sound she made would be muffled. Then she
pounded the arm of her chair and, still careful of her volume,
cursed me. Then she cursed Hal and questioned his species
and parentage. She stared at the blue sky behind the bare
branches until the clarity and beauty there led her away from
her fury. When that had been moved aside, she calmly considered her choices.

She knew Hal was waiting and she didn't want to push the
limit of his patience. Sheila also knew that it would be both
wise and imprudent to hang up the phone. Though she'd been
rather good about saving, she had more than thirty thousand
dollars' worth of new debt and no ready source of income. He'd
mentioned a job, and Sheila could not imagine any help from
that old bully, providence. There would be no unforeseen wind-
falls for Sheila Jericault. Her wisest self, which was wiser now
than it had ever been, was uncomfortably aware that a reunion
with Hal was probably no path to doing good, being a better
person, or happiness. But neither was she a fan of the notion
that poverty and nobility skipped hand in hand down the lane
to virtue. She reasoned that unless she planned to get herself
to a nunnery where she would be sheltered, fed, and clothed,

she would be an ass to walk away from money in a time of need. Besides, she was curious. If she said no, she wouldn't know. What could he possibly want from her now? She let Hal breathe quietly into the phone for a minute more so that he would feel the need to be generous and then said, "Okay. But it'll cost you mucho money."

"Money is not a problem. Make it mucho plus."

"Mucho plus and not a penny less."

"Done."

"Okay. What?"

"Well, it's really very pleasant. Are you on a cordless?"

"No."

"Good."

"Pleasant," Sheila prompted.

"Yes. We feel it would be nice if Polly, uh, had a friend. You know, to keep up with, uh, how she's doing, that sort of thing . . ."

Sheila felt a new anger. "What are you looking for?"

"Nothing," Hal said soothingly. "We hope there's nothing at all. But we do want to keep in touch."

"Indirectly."

"You're a woman."

"So I am."

"Well, that's the whole thing."

"Why?"

"An ounce of prevention."

"Why?" Sheila insisted.

"Angel baby, can't you figure it? The poor man is in *recovery*. The Mrs. is pinning her dirty laundry to the public clothesline, and we don't want any wicked surprises."

Now Sheila was astonished. "Recovery from what?"

"You really have vanished. He checked into the Dorothy B. Sandsworthy clinic two weeks ago. Drugs and alcohol."

"Coxx didn't drink. The man didn't even take aspirin."

Hal moaned. "What does a phoenix rise from?"

"Ashes."

"So we need ashes. Before a man can be cleansed, he has to be soiled, and adultery barely cuts it. He has to be such a fucking mess that every jerk on God's green earth can say, Christ, I'm lucky. At least I'm not that poor son of a bitch. So the story is (and sweetheart, you ought to love this body and soul) that the stress of coping with his, just say for instance, crazy destructive wife who's out to publicly strangle his career, right? understandably leads him to the arms of . . . What's her name? Who could blame this tortured man for seeking a little human comfort? There he was, dealing with the tragically troubled and disturbed and possibly—here's where you can help us out—who knows what else? Where the truth lies? I mean, was she even maybe abusive, neglectful? His poor little children . . . My God. Helpless, all that . . . Poor Kip. Trying to be brave. Dealing with the worst of the worst or whatever the hell while keeping a public image intact and, Lord knows, struggling to be as humane and loving as possible as he tried to protect the boys and bring them up to be Eagle Scouts and all the time nursing a fledgling career in selfless public service because he privately knew what it was to suffer and blah-blah-blah. So all the aforementioned leads him to drink and you name it . . . some nifty addiction to, I don't know, a high-class painkiller, nothing like cocaine, too dirty . . ."

"That's disgusting," said Sheila, who, even as she found herself profoundly repulsed, admired her mentor's heartless artistry and could not help but add to it, as had been her habit for years. "But everybody who knew Kip heard him go on about booze and red meat and his body being a goddamn temple. I can't see addiction is credible here."

"Sheila, pussycat, think. If he himself comes out and admits all this horrible, humiliating shit in public, who's going to call him a liar? Polly? If she does, she'll be discredited. Meanwhile,

Kip passes through the flames, and out he comes. Forged anew. Tempered steel. Complete recovery. Confession. Apology. Pictures of his arms around his smiling kids. Clean. Caring. Different haircut. Twenty pounds thinner. Flat abs. New suits. Maybe Polly'll even forgive him. And if she doesn't, America will. People love forgiving. Makes them feel so goddamn superior. Then, right after he cries on camera, or maybe the happy couple cans el divorcio and renews their vows if we're ultra-lucky, we bring him wide into the national arena. Forget the House. We make him . . ."

"A god among men." Sheila knew what to say. She'd heard enough to understand what had taken hold of Hal. He couldn't stand losing. It was never part of the deal. And having a loss to his record, a stupid loss that never should have happened, even with someone else to blame, hurt. If he transformed Kip, he could snatch victory back from the jaws, from the belly, from the bowels. He could unlose and more. Maybe he could make a President in eight, ten years. That would cheer him up.

"Since you're still up that way and we're in the early stages of what could truly be a landmark—"

"I have no interest in destroying Polly Coxx."

"For chrissake, you're grim. Who's talking about destroying? She's the one sniffling on TV. She's the one with the book deal. Just get to know her. Personally."

"Know her."

Sheila knew what he wanted. She took a sip of the cold coffee beside her. It tasted like poison. But coffee was coffee. She swallowed it anyway.

How Easy It Had Been to Free a Slave

How easy it had been to free a slave. How uplifting. How uncloudy. How absolutely Right. Never mind the thicket of discomfort that had come after. Getting Kiri a decent job wasn't wrong, was it? Sheila asked herself. Never mind, never mind, said Sheila's mind, with a wanton mental selectivity peculiar to only one species on only one planet anywhere. Sheila's own irritation at Kiri was already nearly as good as forgotten, replaced by a longing that spread like a closely knotted but transparent filament net thrown over many things without settling on any one, without making its definitive catch. Over and over she reviewed the first days and hours of Kiri's freedom. So thrilling, so joyful, colorful, clear. Those days defied the season. And now it was most certainly winter. Even indoors, the damp crept under her mohair shawl. The chill forced itself along the seam of her skin, the seam cut and sewn by Hallerman, the man to whom she owed her life. She wrapped her shawl tighter against the aching and the cold and contemplated the agreement she had just made. To search for Polly's vulnerabilities, probe her secrets, if she had them, so that if Hal Orinsek wanted to make use of the knowledge as he worked to gild his tarnished client, he had it ready in his hand. To be her friend, he said, a pleasant job, as if all friend-ships involved a discountable trace of treachery. And Sheila agreed to be her friend. For money. Now what? How easy it had been to free a slave.

It occurred to her to phone Hal back, to refuse the assign-ment. But this she did not do. And so, you might conclude, the story ends. Her seedling soul to be crushed and buried under a mudslide of infamy at some future date. So many times I've seen it. So many times have you. It nearly always involves the taste for means and power that those descended from murder-ous chimpanzees have cultivated over the past five million years. But wait. If you will pardon the expression, have faith.

Aware of her predicament and of her own unwillingness to get out of it, Sheila determined she would find a way to do, if not Good, then at least not harm. And get paid. This way did not come to her instantly. She made some hot tea to fight away the chill and applied herself to the search for a perfect solution. But application was not enough. She needed inspiration. In-spiration sat coyly, there, very much there, but not quite solid and well out of reach, like the moon sparkling in a puddle ready to vanish at the slightest breach of surface tension. She tried this way and that way to coax it toward her, but it was not ready to come.

In exasperation she left her tea and her underheated room and drove to downtown Fallowfield. As it happened, she parked in front of a Realtor's office. As it also happened, by allowing herself the distraction of three hours spent in the en-veloping company of a gray-haired widow who chattered with such vigor that she made magpies seem a taciturn breed, Sheila solved a completely different problem. She saw and rented a tiny stone caretaker's cottage that rested at the edge of a large and rarely occupied estate. It exceeded any hopes she might have had if she'd bothered to have any, and though it was dusty and unfurnished and the windows wanted washing, something about it, maybe its smallness, maybe the fireplace, maybe just the slightly piney smell of the air, felt like a home, not a place to sleep until the next place; a real home, a place to begin, and stay.

When she had filled out the papers and written the check and freed herself of the chattering Realtor, she drove back to look at the place with only her eyes. She hadn't yet a set of keys, so she could not pace the inside a second time that day, but that did not bother her. There would be time for tape measures. She had no real furniture anyway. She had come to see if the feeling would strike her twice. It did. This little house set apart from the road by a low wall of loosely laid stones seemed to have been waiting for her, and she for it. At the back of the house a small forest of neatly planted trees separated the cottage from the main property. Alone beside the house stood a tall sentry pine. The gray trunk rose from a bed of red needles, poking the sky with its barbed spear. She backed away to look at it, stretching her neck until her head could bend no farther back. The tip was laden with clusters of brown. Were they pinecones? she wondered, or more needles, dead yet attached to their sky-scoring branches? Whatever they were, they would fall in time, and Sheila rejoiced to think she would be there to see and know whatever they turned out to be. These sentiments surprised her. They came from a part of herself she had not known. Happily she thought of sleeper sofas and headboards, of weekends spent searching for the right this or that to put on the mantelpiece, and she wondered if the longing she felt might be satisfied by something as simple as a home of her own. And well it might have been. In another time and another life. But at this time and in Sheila's life, a home, while a pleasure and a necessity, was not what her soul quietly, ceaselessly called for, and it was not long before, between picturing sheets and comforters, tablecloths and curtains, her thoughts returned to Kiri Srinvasar and, eventually, to the problem of what to do about Mrs. Polly Coxx.

The Polly Problem

P olly was a problem for a dozen different reasons. From my point of view, the most interesting was probably this: Just as Sheila Jericault had begun to sidle up to the realization that a meaningful human life had certain sticky requirements, goodness being among the stickiest, Polly had cast that notion aside. As she saw it, she'd *been* good. Worshipfully good and loyal and true-blue to her handsome cheating scum of a husband. And what had it got her?

You are undoubtedly waiting for me to remark on graven images and golden calves, for Polly had certainly chosen a false god, but I'll skip that. While I have forever, you don't.

At any rate, Polly had decided to put Polly first, or as she liked to say, "No more Mrs. Nice Girl." Polly had invested much of the advance money for her tell-all, which she called *The Miserable Life of the Political Wife,* in liposuction. And determined to be properly adored as well as adorable, she had invested a good portion of the rest in a full-service (and frequently in-house) personal trainer who was ten years her junior. She had abandoned her clean-cut blond bob for a short, spiky hairdo that, in certain light, looked almost maroon. She had taken to wearing crop-top sweaters that showed her suctioned belly and miniskirts that showed her vacuumed thighs and hideous, expensive purple lizard cowboy boots that showed nothing but rebelliously bad taste.

This was not good news.

The twins were still at school and little George Washington Coxx was napping when Sheila arrived at the tidy Coxx colonial. "It's *my* turn now," explained Polly as she poured her guest a cup of tea. "Sugar? Honey?"

"Honey, thanks." Sheila could not help herself. In her mind she pictured Polly with her rump in the air and her knees folded to her chest, neat on a platter with an apple in her mouth, a feast for Hal, an easy banquet. She sighed, and did not know she had sighed until Polly returned a similar sigh and sat herself at the table.

"You of anyone in the world know what I did for that man."

Sheila nodded. "You were perfect. No one could have asked for more. Kip was such a . . ."

"Fool," said Polly, assuming no other possible end to the sentence. "Exactly." Polly pinged her spoon on the china, causing the tea to slosh into the saucer. "And frankly, I'm so glad you called. I would have called you, but . . ."

Sheila brought her cup to her lips and sipped, burning her tongue on the Constant Comment. "That's okay."

"I gotta show you something," said Polly impulsively. She pushed away her chair and scampered out of the sunny kitchen, which still bore witness to the old Polly with its alphabetized spice rack and home-sewn gingham curtains. "Look," she said, returning with a sheaf of paper. "My researcher—did I tell you I got a researcher?—found all this yummy stuff. See? It puts me in a context, as they say." Polly began to recite. "Counting backward from nowhere in particular, listen to this: Okay, when JFK was in the Senate, his colleagues called him Mattress Jack.

You can figure that out, and everyone knows about whatser-name—the Mafia woman—and Marilyn Monroe. And, um, Aaron Burr, who was Jefferson's VP, he gets married at seventy-seven, right? And his wife is fifty-eight herself, but within a year they're through 'cause he's boffing a few of his clients. Can you believe it? But the good news is, in that case, the day his divorce is granted, the horny coot dies. And, of course, FDR everybody knows about. And the question is, Who *hasn't* had a taste of Bill Clinton's netherbrain? But then he always did admire Kennedy. Alexander Hamilton not only slept with his sister-in-law, there was some other woman whose husband blackmailed him. And listen, even the guy who wrote the 'Star-Spangled Banner' got shot for screwing this congressman's wife while the congressman, Sickles, was meanwhile screwing a prostitute. And Warren G. Harding used to do his honey in the White House closets, which, I gotta tell you, James Buchanan was practically out of. Everyone knew he was gay, only they didn't call it that at the time, and his boyfriend was named King. King and queen. And then there's old Monkey Business Hart challenging the press. And Morris. Whatever. Total testosterone overload. No wonder the country's a mess. They're all too busy fucking, if you'll pardon my . . . And, oh God, Marion Barry with the crack and the prison term, not to mention that little bit on the side—and he gets reelected. As mayor of the nation's capital. Can't forget him. And meanwhile, where are the wives? Half the time they're silent, and the other half the time they're sticking up for these guys. Do you know, me and my researcher think I may be the only one, the only wife in history, to stand up to all this crap loud and clear. Like I said, he'll cheat you like he's cheated me. That's pretty basic. And if that's true, I mean the stuff about me standing up and being the first, it would certainly put me in history and expose that bastard, which is at least something for all my pain and, believe me, sacrifice, and meanwhile I could take care of the boys' financial future. My book has got to be a bestseller, right?"

Sheila was sure she was right. It would be a bestseller and Kip's best weapon against her. There was a reason wives stayed silent, and it had nothing to do with justice. Or loyalty. Sheila smiled as best she could as she prayed, "Oh God, help me." Helplessly imagining the saliva-wetted gleam of Hal's bared teeth and the blood on his sharp carving knife, Sheila forced herself to finish her tea, sipping slowly, stalling. She did not know what to say, and the few extra moments had not delivered inspiration. It had been so easy to free a slave. She settled, for the moment, on silence and was extremely grateful when little George began to cry.

"He's been tugging at his ear," said Polly.

Sheila followed her into the baby's room. "What does that mean?"

"Ear infection." George had pulled himself to his feet and was reaching for his mama. She lifted him up and he wrapped his arms around her neck. "How's my big boy?" George grinned. Polly turned her back toward Sheila so she could see his round face. "It's really mothers that the fate of this world depends on, and our job just gets harder all the time."

Sheila reached out her finger and George squeezed it with unexpected strength, as if to convey a message. Sheila got it. She did not question the source. Who cared? It was inspiration, and that was enough. "You know what I did on the campaign?" she began.

"You were great. Amazing, actually. I always knew that and even Kip . . . I was always telling him . . . I hope you don't think . . . It wasn't even slightly your fault . . . And what I did . . . I mean, you do understand? I devoted myself and then that . . ."

"Would you, in the case, say, of, uh, keeping you and the boys from harm's way, trust my judgment?" Sheila asked carefully.

162

Polly jiggled the baby as she considered what wasn't being said. "Completely," she answered.

"Um . . ."

"You can tell me."

Sheila hesitated. She knew she could not. "Speaking as a friend . . ."

"Go ahead."

"Are you in love with this, um, the cute trainer?"

Polly giggled. "Not really. He's fun. After all the . . ."

"You're not serious or anything?"

"No."

Sheila petted George's tiny fingers. "Exercise is good, nobody can fault fitness, but could you, uh, maybe, and I mean very diplomatically, being sure there are no hard feelings, phase out the . . ."

"S-e-x?"

"He can't spell already, can he?"

Polly laughed. "No. It's a mommy thing. Habit."

"The s-e-x." Sheila touched the baby's cheek, soft as the petal of a pansy, pink as a sunrise.

Polly tilted her head to the side. "Is *he* coming after me?"

Sheila did not answer. For Polly, who had not only been a politician's wife but had been, as Sheila herself had often said, perfect, that was answer enough. She sensed that she was being offered a gift, a gift she could only refuse at her peril. "I have a feeling I should be thanking you."

Sheila nodded up and down, then side to side, a yes and a no at once.

"So much for wild abandon."

"Just for the time being."

"Anything else?"

"Uh . . ."

"The clothes? The hair?"

What impossible luck, she thought. "I would never suggest . . ."

"Okay," said Polly in perfect understanding. "Anything else?"

"Well . . ." Inspiration struck twice! Conclude what you will. "That AIDS fund-raiser you mentioned over tea? The one you read about in the Sunday section? Uh, I'd be delighted to accept your invitation to participate."

"I hate those things," Polly moaned. "Always did."

"I know. And it's all couples. Married men, but . . ."

"I hate married men."

"Let me tell ya."

"Don't," said Polly quietly.

So she knew, thought Sheila. Only seconds before, Sheila had been ready to pop a million imaginary corks and drink to her on-the-spot brilliance. Now she suddenly felt her chest grow hot with shame. "So you'll call later with the details?"

"Sure," said Polly. "Did I read it in the Sunday Lifestyle or the magazine?"

"Lifestyle. And I'm so glad you suggested it. I'm deeply touched by your newfound and public commitment to those who cannot always speak for themselves. And your plan to devote so much of your time . . ."

Polly winked. "Absolutely."

Sheila decided to venture one more suggestion. "And to donate, uh, a portion of your royalties . . ."

Polly squeezed her lips together. Sheila looked at her almost desperately. She did not dare say no. "Have to cover those karmic bets," said Polly smiling the bulletproof smile she had learned at her husband's side.

"Not enough to merely write a check. We gotta show up. Do our part."

"With bells on. And, uh, we'll—I mean, I'll—let it be widely known that I don't want any personal publicity for my good works. That ought to attract some lovely attention." Polly gig-gled. "And annoy the hell out of . . ."

"It'll be a disaster if I give any appearance . . . I mean, I can accept invitations and stuff, that I can do, but I am offici-ally on another, uh, mission . . . I can't help you . . . Not openly . . ." said Sheila.

"Heavens no," said Polly, cuddling her boy. "Do you want to hold him?" she asked.

Sheila actually wanted to do exactly that so much that her shoulder nearly ached at the place where his little head might rest, but she said, "No, I'm afraid I'd drop him or something."

"People worry about the strangest things. You'd never drop him. You're just afraid you might like it. Then what?" Polly smiled as though she had a secret of her own, but she left it at that.

The Affair

Without further word from Sheila, Polly embraced the business of philanthropy with a vigor usually reserved for unscrupulous billionaires who, in a burst of convenient but very tardy conscience, try to ready themselves for some postmortem county fair where only the best-behaved, prettiest pigs get blue ribbons, and the rest are sliced into fatty bacon and fried. (As if the eternal had time for such nonsense.) The difference was: Polly had no thought of buying her way into heaven. Her motive, for the time being, was heartily earthbound. She was simply covering one ass and fighting another. With stunning rapidity, she put away her lizard boots and joined committees She began attending party after party, not for her pleasure—for as you know, she hated that sort of thing—but in order to raise herself above reproach and meanwhile raise lots and lots of money for this or that always indisputably worthy cause.

Sheila was delighted for many of the wrong reasons and a few of the right ones. Whatever, as you mortals say. Whenever. I have observed that those wisest and most courteous among you patiently allow for many lifetimes in which to fold and sort your moral laundry, while a good lot of the rest think it possible to send out with a few piously mumbled words and have it back smelling sweet and on hangers in three hours. From my point of view, Sheila fell in neither category. Her method was indirect. It was, it seems, unknown to her, but she did her own work and her nose was pointed in the right direction, as, for that matter, was Polly's. And they were both doing good.

When Hal called to check on the friendship he had commissioned, Sheila reported on Polly's charities with a weary tone that she did not need to fake, for in addition to moving from the Onthwaites to the cottage, she had attended five benefits in two weeks. "The woman is *possessed*. She had me over there stuffing envelopes on Wednesday, juvenile diabetes, and tonight there's another affair. Heart disease. She tells me they haven't done enough research on women. . . ."

"What did she do? Morph into fuckin' Mother Teresa?" Hal yelled into the phone. Sheila had begun to ask herself the same question, for she had not anticipated Polly's total and instant fervor, but she tried to sound soothing.

She sang a vague and happy song to herself as she dressed for the evening and she was still humming when Polly arrived and tapped her horn.

"What's with you?" said Polly. Sheila smiled and hummed. "You're not in love?"

"Hardly," said Sheila, taking the printed directions from the envelope on the dashboard.

The woman who answered the door was dressed for the occasion but otherwise not what Sheila would have called a natural hostess. She didn't mention her name or ask theirs. She waved to the table where the checks and nametags were being written. She waved to the steel coatrack that had been jammed into the entry hall. "Food's this way," she said, flicking her wrist to the left and heading right.

"Nice," said Polly.

"Very," said Sheila.

They paid, and pasted their nametags in the usual place. "You can always tell a doctor's house by its total impersonality," said Polly. "They decorate the life right out of them." Polly took a neat oval of tekka maki from a silver tray. When she was finished chewing the gummy rice and papery seaweed and the red raw tuna, she swallowed and added, "Or their wives do. Tastefully, of course."

"Or their wives do what tastefully?" asked Sheila. She had been led away, into a tiny heaven, by the two crisply fried oysters she had just finished, and she wanted to return without delay. "Have you tried these?"

Sheila saw a waiter clear what had to be the kitchen door with a tray, a tray full of what her mouth desired. "Let's go," she whispered, as if she were a commando on a raid. She took Polly's elbow and sidled through the crowd of people, eyes only on the oysters. She witnessed a hand plucking the last of paradise off the white paper doily. "Shit."

"Never mind," said Polly, handing Sheila a potato pancake with a dab of sour cream in the center. "Have this with a little caviar."

Sheila handed it back. "I'm obsessed with these oysters."

Polly ate the potato pancake. "So is everyone else."

Another smaller tray of oysters emptied almost before Sheila noticed them. "We didn't stand a chance."

Polly gave her a nudge. "Outsmart them. Go in the kitchen and nab a plateful before the waiter gets out the door. I'll meet you."

"Get out of here."

Polly reached for a paper plate and handed it to Sheila. "Don't be a sissy. Besides, you got to respect your obsessions."

"What the hell," said Sheila, pushing through the swinging kitchen door, which whacked her in the rear as it swung shut.

She jumped. No one noticed. A waiter sat at a table rapidly stacking vegetables and dip. Beside him, the woman who had greeted them at the door sliced thick slabs of tekka maki. "Are you in charge of those amazing oysters?" asked Sheila.

The vegetable waiter leaped up and dashed out the door as a waitress with an empty tray entered and assumed a waiting pose. "Gimme a sec," the woman said as if the silent girl were rushing her. Then she answered Sheila. "Wish I could take credit. They're his. And he won't give me the recipe." She tilted her head in the direction of the sink.

A man with graying hair stood rinsing silvery oysters in a colander. He gave the colander a gentle shake and spread the oysters one by one across a cookie sheet filled with a layer of something that looked like speckled pancake batter. He flipped them and tossed them into a black iron pan and flipped them again almost as soon as they'd touched the oil. Seconds later he lifted the oysters out of the pan and set them on a paper towel.

"Great," said the woman, suddenly whisking the towel away and dumping the hot oysters on the waiting waitress's empty tray. The object of Sheila's desire vanished before she could seize even one. The door swung open and shut. The woman grabbed her sliced tekka maki and followed the girl out, fleeing toward the hungry guests on the next swing.

"I better work on my reflexes," Sheila said to the man at the sink.

The man laughed. "Wouldn't help."

"They're pretty damn fast," said Sheila. "But now I know you." She noticed his face for the first time. "And you're the guy with the goods."

"That I am," he said, smiling and wiping his hands on a greasy apron. He sipped a glass of ice water. "Hot work, oysters."

It was not the first time Sheila had seen that face. His hair was thick and straight and almost too boyish the way he wore it. She imagined he just didn't think about it one way or another. He was a bit pudgy and probably didn't think about that, either. There he was, not perfect but charming and more than that, especially as he leaned for a moment's rest on the kitchen counter. Sheila wondered at his age. Maybe forties. Maybe older. His beard made it hard to tell. His brows and lashes were thick and black. His eyes, smallish eyes, were blue, even deeper than she'd remembered, blue on the verge of lavender. "I know you," said Sheila, feeling as if time had folded in upon itself so that the months that had passed since she'd depended on the reassuring beauty of his eyes had vanished, and Then and Now were one. "I not only know you, I love you. Because you saved my life. You're Hallerman."

"That I am."

"What in God's name are you doing here?"

Thinking not at all of my name, Hallerman stared at the pretty woman who had just declared her love. "Well," he began, wanting to stall until he figured out what part of what she said he might respond to. "Yes." It would be rude to ask for her name, and the shoulder strap of her purse covered her name-tag. Her name would certainly connect her to the procedure she claimed had saved her life. It would certainly help. As he thought about it, he did rather remember her. Not distinctly. He had a sense she had been an emergency. Beautiful hair, red-gold like an autumn leaf. She had freckles that lightly suggested themselves and beautiful eyes. Like his. He had a brief sensation, looking at them, that he was looking at himself, in his own eyes, seeing himself contained in another's face. "I am here because this is my house." He could say that much. Usually, especially with an emergency patient, Hallerman didn't look much at the face. What he saw was a jumble of white sheeting and green plastic, skin to be cut, muscle to be moved, and blood. He saw monitors and clamps. He saw what needed to be done. The face was an irrelevance to him. He might see the face postop, but by then he'd usually lost interest. The job was done. "Yes." Now, maybe, he had it. "You were my AVM." He remembered now that she had come too close. That he had almost lost her. "That was a wild one."

Sheila stared at his face intensely. How should she feel toward the man who had led her to this confusion? There was no answer, even, to this. Love, yes. But something else, gratitude and ingratitude, pressing against each other with equal force. "You saved my life," she repeated.

Hallerman blushed. "Not me alone. How are you?" He found himself really wanting the answer.

Sheila knew it. She took some trouble looking for the words that could come closest to the truth. "I don't know yet. All kinds of ways." Sheila shrugged. She wanted to say more but didn't know how to express how complicated the more was, and she feared that if she got going, he'd think she was an idiot.

The woman and the waitress slammed back through the door. "Honey, where are my oysters?" said the woman.

"I was taking a break," said Hallerman.

"Well, it's over." The woman yanked open the refrigerator door and dropped a plate of sliced fruit into the ready hands of the waitress. She pulled a tray of miniature spinach pies from the oven, arranged them in a green and gold spiral and pirouetted out the door again.

"I've been derelict in my duties," Hallerman explained.

"My fault," said Sheila.

"Completely. I take no responsibility."

"Is she your wife?"

"Yes," said Hallerman. Sheila watched him open and loosen a half dozen oysters from their shells with an extraordinary deftness. "Well, sort of." He slid five of the oysters into the colander and put the sixth in his mouth. "Not exactly." He swallowed it. "No." He took a raw oyster from the colander and held it out to Sheila.

She shook her head. "I'll wait. But I want a whole bunch before *she* gets hold of them."

"My wife?"

"You tell me. People tend to know if people are their wives, Doctor."

"It's complicated. I've been married before. Twice. And the first time I gave my wife half of what I had, which was a lot at the time, and the second time I gave my wife half, which was less after giving away half once before. So then I was left with a quarter of whatever I would have had if I had stayed married in the first place. So Carol and I are skipping the marriage bit." He filled the colander with the oysters he'd shucked while explaining his life. Now he patted the oysters under a light trickle of water. "Because things can happen." He dumped the lot in the batter and spread the oysters with the back of a spoon.

Sheila examined the pile of shells, hoping she might accidentally find a pearl. "Things can happen? Does she fall for that?"

"What an impertinent question to ask your surgeon," said Hallerman. Then he was silent, tending to his exquisite oysters. Setting eight on Sheila's paper plate and covering them with a napkin to absorb the grease, he added, "Hide these."

Sheila picked up her plate and kissed Hallerman quickly on the lips. "Thanks," she said, and then, after she was well out the door and had split the oysters four and four with Polly, she wondered how she could have been so bold. She answered herself and swallowed the perfect oysters, forgetting, after all that, to taste them as they went down. She wanted to kiss him again.

Before Hallerman went to bed that night, he thought about Sheila. It would be easy to get her name. Why did he want her name? Just curiosity, he decided, contenting himself with what he knew was a lie.

Carol was happy. "It was a total success," she said as she emerged from the bathroom combing her wet hair without looking in the mirror. She rummaged in her dresser and found her favorite torn T-shirt and squiggled into it. Hallerman picked up a magazine from the night table. He did not want to read it, but he opened it as if he did. Carol leaned across the pages, tickling his chest with her wet hair. She kissed him, but he felt Sheila's lips.

Hallerman let go of the magazine and held Carol for a moment, not too long, not so she'd think he wanted anything more, and said, "You did a great job tonight. As usual."

"I just wish you'd break down and give me that recipe."

"No way," said Hallerman. "Then I'd have to leave the kitchen and mingle with the goddamn guests."

Carol sniffed a laugh. She snuggled against his ribs in her favorite place under his arm and closed her eyes. Hallerman closed his, not wanting to look at Carol fondly or any other way.

He couldn't bear to. He already knew what he wanted and what he was going to do. He knew it absolutely, as a question answered beyond reason. His certainty frightened him, but he did not want to stop himself. Not at all.

Faith and Infidelity

He was happy with Carol, happy enough. Carol had nothing to do with it. It was Sheila, Sheila in particular. As I said, Hallerman knew that he would, would and must, embrace Sheila Jericault. And that was that.

He had to kiss the perfect scarlet incision he himself had made, to enter and unite with the body he had saved, her body. His heart knew this and, those cynics among you might add, so did the part of him made for the job, but it was his soul that compelled him, and he let it.

What of his commitment to Carol? I have nothing to say about that. Though you might expect otherwise, I was sympathetic toward the mysterious power of Hallerman's sudden desire. For if I should happen to notice when one of you reaches for another in ill-planned inexplicable love, leaping without consideration for the duration of the fall or the consequences of landing, I see a soul bound by blind courage and foolishness to expand at any cost. I see faith in something that cannot be wholly known by the mortal mind, and as I rejoice, I weep.

He telephoned. She answered as if she had been expecting

his call. He came to her cottage. She offered him tea, which neither of them drank, and made a fire that burned evenly in perfect reds and oranges and blues. Without much in the way of conversation—what was there, really, to say?—they began.

All animals mate, and it is not likely that you will ever know how swans feel or what it means to elephants or if rabbits swoon in rabbit love as they join together, male and female. You probably assume they feel nothing, it means nothing, that there can be no rabbit love. Yours is a vain species. But then, they—the swans and elephants and rabbits—certainly do not understand your ways, nor does any other creature on earth. And to be entirely candid, we who have sprung from your mind and other sources well beyond it, having vast data upon which to draw, are stymied along with the rest of Creation.

Nonetheless, this is what I witnessed in the case of Hallerman and Sheila: In motion, up and down and in and out, they did nothing different from what other humans do when they do this sort of thing; however, it happened that through this outwardly mundane physical union, the two breached the boundaries of each other's skin, transcending the confinement of their bodies without effort, and found a vast and nameless place to be.

How did it feel? For Sheila, thus: as though she'd been cut open once again, this time at her heart, and Hallerman had reentered there and wherever else he willed, again and again, deep into the dark and red, so that she felt him everywhere inside her, and his ecstatic pleasure was indistiguishable from her own; it was hers and she felt it in her body.

She had never known such communion. Nor had he. When their bodies drew apart, they had no disposition toward conversation.

What could there possibly be to say?

When the silence began to seem too long, Sheila offered him

tea once more, and though he accepted her offer, she did not bother to make it.

She stayed in his arms and he hummed a tune she recognized but could not identify.

Time had been beyond their notice or care but it had also passed. Hallerman leaned over the bed and reached for his watch where it had fallen on the floor. He checked the hour. "Oh my God," he said. It was time for him to go. He was expected here and obliged there. He had surgery at seven. And so he had to go, out of the cottage and out of her to Elsewhere, where she wasn't. "I wish I could stay," he whispered in her ear. He reached for a blanket and wrapped her in it. The red fringe tickled her neck. Her cheeks were raw from the roughness of his beard, and her lips were swollen from his kisses. She held the blanket closed at her breasts and watched until his green Jeep vanished. "I should go to the grocery," she said to herself, but she did not want to be anywhere but where she was. Slightly hungry, she returned to the rumpled bed that smelled of love and let herself travel serenely from one dream to another until the morning sun passed through the pines and warmed her eyelids.

Rose Polish

T hat morning and ever after, Sheila remembered the extraordinary state of total communion that she and Hallerman had achieved without intent or effort. She remembered it with a feeling of reverence and awe, and had to content herself with remembering, for though their carnal pleasure in each other was immense, it was never to be quite *that* way again. It could not be. The reason was plain to me. Perhaps it will be plain to you.

You see, the first time they came together, it was as the lifesaver and the dying, saved from death. There was no other purpose to their meeting as they did, over blood. Because of it, Sheila, who had tasted death, owed Hallerman her life. Hallerman, too, had a debt, though it was unacknowledged and harder to name. He owed Sheila his gratitude for having been a life that he could save, for saving lives was his salvation and he knew in his heart that it was often Grace and not his skill that made the difference between living and dying. Certainly, he and she might have gone through their lives without meeting again, with only the slightest sense of something missing, but that is not what happened.

Usually, the debt of life to life and life to death is acknowledged and paid, if at all, by symbol and perhaps some attendant and somewhat abstracted ritual, but again, that is not what happened. This time, it was made real and thus pleased all the gods who took notice on that day, not only me.

Joining their bodies as they did, lifesaver and life saved, they became as air to air or water to water or life to life and death, indivisible from the whole of everything. And at the same time, uniting, they put an end to their unity as a mother who has carried a child within her body and shared with it her blood then cannot keep it inside. She must sever the body tie—it is the rule of nature—set the child free and see him separate in his skin and his hungers, or see the end of them both.

It did not feel like an end to Sheila Jericault and Hallerman. They felt that their union heralded some sort of magnificent beginning, perhaps a lifesaving of another sort. I will not comment except to say that they were mortals and wished as ever mortals do to cling to the profound (as if it could be held in place), and so neither wanted to think that what had happened once was a vapor now, a breath exhaled. They drew new breaths and continued reaching for each other in eagerness and hope. Again and again they embraced in a different joy and more intensely, striving, though neither said a word of it, to relive that other union, which done was also gone. And so the completed circle of lifesaver and life saved metamorphosed into an idea, a wisp and a fact that was true but could not be grasped twice. To each other they became man and woman and just that, which was both a simpler and a harder thing.

As man and woman they lived in the world, and that contained not only their bond and their joys but Hallerman's schedule, which was filled with many lives to save. It contained Hallerman's accounting of two failed marriages. It contained Carol, with whom he shared his bed and his meals. It also contained Carol's little daughter, Sue, whom he had not fathered but probably loved more than anyone in the world, including Sheila.

Though he thought of her as he cut skin, blood, and muscle with a sure hand and a knife, and he dreamed of her as he drank coffee, as he made love to Carol, and as he drove Sue to soccer, picturing her as his invisible companion, his companion in spirit and desire, Hallerman saw Sheila only when he could fit her in. And Sheila, full of love and wishes, told herself she didn't mind.

But she spent a great portion of her day yearning for him and wondering about questions that were not hers to answer. How could she know if he would ever leave Carol? Sheila felt the need of a friend.

While she and Polly drove from bank to bank collecting boxes of nonperishable food for the Help Your Neighbor Foundation, she tried to find some way to speak about her love affair. But she couldn't, for at least three reasons, and she didn't. She busied herself playing with baby George and sorting cans of food by contents, and it was then, or about then, that she decided it was time, that is, she was ready, to look up Kiri Srinvasar. In her mind the matters were unconnected, but as you know, a mind does not always feel bound to tell the truth, even to itself. When the beans were with the beans and the soup was with the soup and the pasta was sorted by shape, Sheila and Polly loaded the car one more time. "I don't feel like cooking," said Polly. "Do you want to come for pizza tonight? We could talk about the clothing drive."

"No," said Sheila. "I can't." She spread her fingers for Polly's examination. "I'm desperate for a manicure."

Sheila knew where to go. She'd known for a while. She just hadn't had the courage to see Kiri's face. Now she drove to Dahlia's Nails in East Farbury without any fear at all, for her mind was occupied by the feel, the look, the touch, and the circumstances of Hallerman. She saw Kiri right away and her heart quickened. Though Kiri, who was known as Kathy to the girls in the shop, had a customer, she jumped up. "My dear dear friend Sheila has come at last finally," she cried. "I am so utterly very very very delighted at the sight of you!"

"Me, too," said Sheila, and she was. When Kiri was finished with her customer, Sheila took her place across the table and Kiri took her hand, placing it in a bowl of warm bubbles. "How have you been?"

"Oh, fine fine fine," said Kiri. "Very fine."

"And how are things at the Wicketts'?"

"Very very very very fine," Kiri answered, pushing at Sheila's cuticles with an angled wooden stick. Kiri's own well-manicured hands showed no scars now. Her purple lipstick was the only reminder of bruising, but her lips smiled. And her painted face showed nothing of the cruelty she had known. She wore eight jeweled rings at once and a gold watch with a face encircled by diamonds. Her ornaments flashed in the light and cast moving rainbows onto the wall. "And how are things in the living of your life?"

"Well," Sheila began. "There is a man . . ." And she went on from there, pausing only to choose a rose pink polish for her nails, as Kiri nodded and filed and painted and listened.

"Ah . . ." she said, as if she understood the matter in depth and approved of it entirely. When she did not say ah, she nodded over and over in the same manner that Sheila had so recently found unbearable, saying, "Yes, yes, very good, very very good, a very good sign," which was exactly what Sheila wanted to hear.

Sheila nodded in return. Kiri rubbed lotion into her hands and made them soft. Then Sheila paid, adding a fifty percent tip for Kiri, and said, "I've missed you. We must make this a regular thing."

"Yes yes," answered Kiri eagerly. "I would be so very happy

at that indeed, and the rose polish suits you very very much. The men like pink. He will be most delighted."

Sheila looked at her ten shining fingernails. They were beautiful. Flawless. She did not put on her gloves for fear of spoiling them. As she walked to her car, her fingers began to sting from the chill and she wiggled them like a pianist playing an imaginary melody on unseen keys. She looked back toward Dahlia's and waved. Kiri was free. Kiri was happy. And everything was very very very very fine. Sheila paused to think about that. Was everything very very very very fine? She felt some responsibility. It was she who had turned Kiri out into the world. And she had seen for herself that Kiri's relationship to what others might call the truth was often no more than that between nodding acquaintances. As I say, she paused, feeling the bond between herself and the slave she had freed, realizing that in its own way it was as strong as that between herself and Hallerman. Attached here, attached there, more than attached, bound tight, soul to soul. Was Kiri really all right? That was all too much to contemplate on a street corner. She dismissed the impulse toward further reflection. Very very very very fine was fine with her. Why doubt it? Why pry? And then she thought of the jeweled rings and the diamond-faced watch. Perhaps they were fake, she thought, knowing that Kiri would never stand for that. Then where did they come from? She refused to wonder. There was no way to wonder about that without taking on a lot of other wondering as well. She told herself she did not want to know more—Kiri had *said* she was fine, and that ought to be enough—and returned to her comforting cottage. There she waited with perfect rose pink nails for her lover with the violet eyes to call her on the telephone.

Kiri and the Jewels

L et us leave Sheila where she remained, waiting, waiting for days, her heart cut open, feeling raw and sad and more alive than when she'd felt nothing and liked it that way. You will not be missing much if I change the subject for a while. As it happened, her rose polish was chipped by the time Hallerman called and gone by the time she saw him next. This, because he was busy tending to one emergency after another, and he could not nor did he want to get away. He knew that when he was in the hospital, he was usually doing, if not always the right thing, then something that he could call good. He could not call making love to a woman who was not Carol good, though it always felt good when he did it and he had no wish to stop. Being in the hospital kept him out of the muddle he had created, so he stayed there as long as he could. Anywhere else, he had to lie. And when he lied, to Sheila and to Carol, he was always believed, and loved all the more, loved like a treasure, which made it worse.

And so we come to Kiri and the jewels.

There is no answering the questions Sheila was loath to entertain without answering other questions, also unasked, about the Wicketts, particularly young Boggy.

Bob's rage was as it had been, and his gun was always ready. He dreamed of his shooters at night and thought of them all day. But ever since Clint Eastwood's amber-skinned woman had come by some miracle to live in his house, Boggy had been in love.

Though he did not go around saying it in words and certainly not to his dad, all the kids at school suspected something, and his silence only enhanced their suspicions. Boggy was different, and the difference about him bumped up his status several notches. Every girl in his class developed an eye for him, not knowing why he had all of a sudden become attractive. Boggy didn't seem to notice the whispering clusters of girls who twittered as he sauntered past in his new kind of Clintish cowboy way and he didn't seem to care. Though he might have been permitted to walk hand in hand across the schoolyard with even the stunning Christy Barnett, he walked alone, choosing none of his willing classmates, not one, not even once.

That caused things to turn quickly. His mystique began to make them angry. The girls wondered, If not her and not her and not me, then who? Their whispered admiration evolved into whispered hate. "Who the hell does he think he is?" they wondered.

But Boggy paid no more attention to their resentment than he had to their adoration. He loved Kiri, and that was enough for him. His love for Kiri felt more compelling and complicated than any feeling Boggy had ever known, and it felt good. Feeling good had been way too rare around his house since his dad got shot and until Kiri came—for which he offered a zillion silent thanks to that Sheila woman—Boggy had feared that being so out of practice, he might be sad forever. Instead, there was this: a kind of wanting, love, desire that was unimaginably his and new. He was almost thirteen and so, so dizzily hot with it.

Too often for his comfort, Bob Wickett felt aroused in the presence of Kiri Srinvasar. He did not dare pursue his sexual urges, so he anxiously brushed them away when they came, avoiding the traveling spark, keeping a careful space between himself and the beautiful amber woman who lived and slept in his house. He had no idea his young son was aflame. He noticed some attitude thing. As he saw it, Boggy was kind of off somewhere strange, but not strange-in-love, just strange-strange and he'd changed in a way Bob couldn't say he liked. He would have felt more comfortable if there was some wise-mouthing going on. That, he could understand. He would have chalked up a little extra guff to getting teenage. But what made Bob itchy was the same mysterious air that bugged the kids at school. Boggy had gone quiet.

At first Bob thought it was his fault, figuring he had gone overboard on the overtime at the dairy. With Kiri so handy and helpful and all, it was easy to add on those hours, try to catch up on the finances, maybe close the whopping hole in his bank account. Bob knew he was too wrapped up in himself, cared too damned much about money, never mind revenge, which he damn well meant to get, but when he cut back a couple of days for the boy's sake so they could be together, Boggy didn't feel like it.

Bob took him to Burger King. He said, "Go whole hog. Order anything you want."

Boggy ordered a lot and Bob had hope, but then the boy wolfed his food and jiggled his knee impatiently, suffering openly while Bob tried to draw out the time, make the wires connect, make conversation.

Finally, Boggy said, "Dad, I think I want to get back home."

So Bob let him drive. He didn't say a word when the boy went a little fast. He didn't know what to say. He prayed there'd be a western on that he and his boy might watch together. When they got home, he studied the *TV Guide* and found one.

"Hey, Boggy," he said. "We got *High Noon* on Five tonight. How 'bout it? I'll do up some popcorn. You melt the butter."

Boggy headed up the stairs. "Nah," he said. "I'm sick of Gary Cooper."

Sick of Gary Cooper! Bob let it go. He didn't bother to make the popcorn. Just sat alone in his sagging chair. *High Noon* was *High Noon*. Some things were sacred. Boggy, he decided, was just being a jerk. So let him, he thought, and put the boy out of his mind. He cleaned his gun and thought about how simple justice was. In the Old West. Not now; now it was just words, a chant on the news. Everybody wanted it. Nobody got it.

It was quiet upstairs. Bob heard the shower running and the usual buzz of Kiri's TV shopping shows. Bob had hated his own dad. Boggy didn't hate him. He wanted to keep it that way, so he told himself, Leave the boy be, and got himself one Budweiser, then a second.

In the bathroom, the water from the shower drummed against the tile, but Boggy had not stepped under it. He stood naked under the fluorescent light, remembering. That morning before school he'd seen Kiri. *Seen* her. Kiri always put on a robe when she woke up, belting it tight over her nightgown. She came downstairs in her fuzzy slippers and set breakfast on the table before she took the time to dress. That was the way she always did it. Boggy would have his eggs and toast or whatever he was having that day, and she'd head back upstairs. When she was all done up, she'd sit at the table with him, sipping tea, smiling, waiting quietly for him to finish so she could clear the dishes. That morning, Boggy sat down, same as he always did, but he spilled half a glass of orange juice down the front of his chamois shirt. He said, "Shit," and pulled his shirt off, but it was too chilly to stay bare chested. He left the table and went up to his room for something else to wear and, passing the bathroom, on the one day he did something different, he saw Kiri step from the shower. *Saw* her.

Boggy went through his day from class to class seeing Kiri, only Kiri, Kiri when the teachers spoke, Kiri on the blackboard, Kiri in the cafeteria. Again and again in his mind he slowed the few magnificent seconds, trying to examine them more closely, see more than he'd actually seen, the blur of brown wetness, the pitch of her shoulders, the swing of her breasts, the shocking black of her nipples, the white towel between her legs. He studied the detail, adding what he could not find. Now, with the water running, his eyes closed, the steam making sweat on his cheeks, he saw her black nipples again and imagined them tasting like sweet raisins. He tasted the taste as if it were real and imagined more. He saw the muscles in her calf as she stepped onto the bath mat. Moving the mat under his own feet, feeling the plush with his toes, he grabbed himself and began to match the vision, the bits of her, with a rhythm; and doing this, he pretended it was her hand that drew the heat to a point and not his own.

And then—he did not know how it had happened, he did not ask—it was her hand. Kiri moved his fingers away, seizing the rhythm. Her fingers owned him. He gasped, ashamed, afraid, but not willing to stop. He dared not open his eyes. What if it wasn't real? What if it was? He yielded. As his knees buckled, he knocked his elbow against the metal hinge of the shower door. He yelped. Kiri giggled at his pain, so he almost believed that she was real and she was there and she had done what she had done. "You are bleeding, boy," she said in the same slightly impatient voice she might have used if he'd fallen off his bicycle in the midst of attempting a stupid trick. "Rinse yourself off."

Kiri left the bathroom quite pleased with her first effort at handling the strangely capped column of pink flesh. Through half-closed doors, she had seen the eldest Babahani boy rub this part of himself and noted its effect upon his mood. From this remembered observation came useful inspiration and its employment in the service of a most superb and efficient idea for expanding her good fortune. Already she sensed that the result of her bold grasp of Boggy Wickett would be well worth the price of her embarrassment and mild revulsion. And from her point of view, she remained unspoiled, for she remained unentered and, thus, a virgin.

Boggy stepped into the shower, where he stood in a half-trance until the water got cold, watching the red flow down his arm and off his fingers.

When Boggy was dry and dressed, he opened the bathroom door quite carefully, as if he expected that everything outside would be strange to him, as if the floor might be air and the air solid. But there were no surprises, no signs that the entire universe had changed, though from his point of view (and that of your chaos theory—for if a butterfly in flight can alter the weather on earth, what can a jet of sperm shot fast through still air do?), it had.

Kiri's bedroom door was shut. He stood outside, listening to a cheery voice he had heard every night since the day his beloved Kiri had arrived. "And now Beverly is modeling a lovely diamond tennis bracelet," said the voice. "Smashing, Beverly! What? Hurry ladies! To those phones! The number is right there on the screen. I'm told there are only two hundred of these lovely diamond tennis bracelets left, so don't break your own heart and mine."

"Two hundred!" he heard Kiri murmur in response and then he heard her on the phone, ordering in her delicate voice, or he thought he did. How could he be sure? He touched the gash on his elbow. There was his evidence, he thought, real blood, a real cut, evidence of Kiri Srinvasar's love.

The next morning, after no sleep, Boggy took his place at the table. There she was. The same robe. The usual gown. Her good-morning was no different from any other good-morning she had uttered to him. He glanced at her hands and felt himself grow hard in his jeans. With his eyes cast down, he set to buttering his toast. All night he had whispered, "Kiri, Kiri, Kiri," into the darkness. In daylight, he did not seem to be able to bring himself to speak at all. She poured his coffee. He forced himself. "Thank you," he said. Kiri nodded. She left the kitchen. Then quickly she returned. She touched her fingers to her lips and then touched the boy's cheek. "I was perhaps thinking that I might enjoy some very high hopes that you would help me with the tiniest little project, don't you think? And it would be our very lovely little secret. Wouldn't that be nice?"

Boggy agreed it would. He did not ask what the project might be, nor did he care. Whatever Kiri wanted, he would do it. He would do anything and no less than everything. For her. If she wanted. If it pleased her. If he could hope that she might touch him even once again, again, again, there.

In your world, the technical term for Kiri's little project was credit card fraud, though Kiri would have been insulted beyond words if anyone had ever described her activities in that way. To Kiri, it was a way to embrace delight. It was wisdom, inspired wisdom, a duty performed in service to the gods who had so honored her and the destiny that had been revealed to her by her great friend Sheila Jericault.

Kiri tended her gratitude with considerably more conscientious care than I tend most of you. She was, in this way, an example to us all in the heavens and on earth, or so she intended to be in order to prove herself worthy of her new and soon to be exalted position. She did not forget that it was Sheila who had released her from cruel servitude and Sheila who had brought her to the Marriott pool, where as a goddess she dined, and as a goddess she floated in tranquil ecstasy. It was dear Sheila who had shown her how very very much there was to need, how many adornments might be had, and it was Sheila who had presented the small golden plastic card, her inspiration, American Express, Visa, MasterCard. Yes! It had been revealed by Sheila. That Kiri herself should be denied such a card because, as Sheila had kindly explained to her, the law would not permit her to work legally, surely this was wrong, an obstacle placed in her way so that she might prove her nobility and further worthiness by overcoming it.

With gratitude, she understood that her work as a manicurist had been another blessing. At Dahlia's she had been required to learn the ways of all the many cards, and she handled them day after day. All the women whose fingers she stroked, whose nails she painted, used their cards to become as beautiful as it was possible for them to be, and Kiri had determined that having no card of her own, she was meant to use their cards and when that became unwise, then other cards, for the same and greater purposes. All the signs were present.

Kiri chided herself for having been so foolishly reluctant when Sheila had showed her the way, bringing her to the Wickett household. In Sheila's wisdom, she led Kiri not only to the Wicketts but to Dahlia's and the knowledge of golden cards, et cetera. Without Sheila, she would not have had Boggy, who now belonged to her; and was it not true that, as she had hoped, the young Boggy, with his ardent worship of her very self and his fortunate ability to drive, made possible even wider and greater achievement of the having of wonderful, wondrous *things*.

Kiri charged whatever destiny intended for her pleasure, whatever her heart knew to be its need, using the credit card numbers she had obtained at work, in garbage cans, on the street, and elsewhere. Knowing that the law of man can differ from the law of gods, she often ordered her treasures from the pay telephones outside Grimaldi Drug or from some other secret place. Sometimes she had Boggy drive to a phone at an abandoned gas station, and there, too, she might or might not favor him again with her divine touch. Sometimes—if, for instance, a particular jewel might be snatched up by another caller if she did not take immediate possession—she abandoned her precautions and made telephone orders from the house. She never ordered from work. There, she performed her tasks neatly and quickly and made Dahlia extremely happy by doing so. Work was for the gathering of direct and indirect knowledge that might be of use. Each customer's home address was kept on an index card along with nail color preferences and personal information so that as the manicurist worked, her conversation might be filled with the things that most mattered— friends, husbands, birthdays and anniversaries, so on. Kiri found that it was no trouble at all to arrange for an unsuspicious delivery of even the most valuable emerald if the parcel was sent directly to the cardholder's billing address. And if one was blessed with the devoted aid of a clever and desperately willing white boy who might retrieve the parcels from this mailbox or that without notice, how very very very very lovely. If her joy were not enough with all this loveliness at hand, Kiri soon realized that when she spent none of her own money, what she had earned by her hands was easily saved and rapidly accumulated here in Connecticut, America, the great land of endless more.

As she lay in her bed with her jewels under her pillow, Kiri often thought of floating in time and eternity—beside Sheila and her mother and her beloved sisters and perhaps even her sisters' children—once more in that sparkling viperless pool of colorless water that was neither hot nor cold.

And Kiri went along in this very very very fine way for a long enough time that her pillow became hard, lumpy, and for all the wealth within it, horribly uncomfortable. Since Kiri had need of a good night's sleep, she was quick with a practical solution. However, on the very afternoon she had ordered a second pillow, of finest goose down, to lay over the first, there was an incident, as there so often is.

It was not a Dahlia's day, so Kiri was at home. She had stripped Bob's and Boggy's beds and taken down the curtains to be washed. She vacuumed the whole upstairs and scrubbed the tiles in the bathroom. She emptied all the wastebaskets into a plastic garbage bag and carried the bag downstairs. She wandered into the kitchen, which was where, if her mind was elsewhere, she tended to go without thinking. There was always something to be done in the kitchen. Kiri turned the toaster upside down in the sink. She found herself in the mood for a top-to-bottom, corner-to-corner scouring of the sort Mrs. Babahani always insisted must be done. She rarely did that kind of cleaning now. Bob and Boggy did not require spotlessness. Good enough was good enough for them, and that was usually good enough for her. In spite of the clear sky and the warming sun, she found the Mrs. occupying her thoughts. In the past, she had avoided thinking of the Mrs. What was the use of it? she would ask herself whenever her mind strayed. But on this day, her thoughts were not bitter and painful, but of a rather tender cast. She missed the Mrs. and her cruelty. "Odd," said Kiri out loud to herself, but then she decided her thoughts were not as odd as all that. The Mrs. was cruel, yes, but she appreciated thorough cleanliness. She knew perfection when she saw it, and she expected nothing less. And thus, she knew the value of Kiri's work and appreciated it as the Wicketts never would. If her thoughts had stopped at that point, perhaps Kiri's mind would not have turned down the unlit road, blending shadows until there was nothing but darkness even in daylight, perhaps the day itself would have been different. But Kiri persisted, picturing the Mrs.'s smooth, long-fingered hands. Her own were no less perfect now. No more cuts or calluses, no dirty crevices or peeling skin. Her hands were soft and small, her nails even and neat. Kiri tore open a new box of yellow latex gloves and smelled the fingers. To protect her delicacy, she always replaced them at the slightest sign of wear or rubbery stench. She loved new yellow gloves, and Bob Wickett never questioned the expense. The Mrs. never would have allowed such extravagance. In the service of the Mrs., she worked gloveless until her knuckles bled. And now? As a slave, she had craved rest and kindness most of all. And now?

Kiri thought of the boy; was he not her slave? And was she not kind to give him the chance to earn her favor, though she sometimes laughed at him cruelly, asked ever more and more, withheld her touch, and granted it reluctantly, with ceremony, as the Mrs. had once granted her one extra hour's sleep? How gratefully Kiri had received her sleep; and now, did not her kind touch mean more to the boy because he suffered to receive it? She asked herself these questions. Intoxicated by the dark liquor of her thoughts, she compared human cruelty to a godlike trait, mistaking divine indifference or distraction for the base and dangerous malice for which mankind has only itself to thank. Was she not as a goddess, dispensing her most beautifully cruel and perfect love without mercy or weakness? Oh yes yes yes, very much *so,* she answered to her own delight. She loved power as no god need do, and loved it wildly. *He* begged to please. *She* was the master. It seemed a wonderful justice to her. "The Mrs. is my sister now," said Kiri. She squirted liquid Ivory into a plastic bucket. Even I was in awe as her speculation continued: Is not slavery the ultimate evil? she asked herself, answering, yes. For the slave, yes. For the slaveholder? Oh yes, slavery was always an evil. But also no. The slaveholder and others, perhaps many others, had the benefit of the slave's hard work, and the slave would learn to be truly grateful for even the smallest relief or kindness. Did she not know more than most that kindness judiciously dispensed brought a greater profit than kindness that flowed freely? Kiri dropped a sponge in the soap and filled the bucket until it was so heavy she could barely hoist it out of the sink. The suds sloshed across the floor. Kiri pulled the caked burners off the stove and the grimy racks from the oven. She lay them on the kitchen counter before she dipped her yellow-gloved hands into the soapy bucket and found the waterlogged sponge at the bottom. So much to do. To my relief, she abandoned her thoughts and lost herself in scrubbing and scrubbing, striving to remove every evidence of dirt, if not for the Wicketts, then in homage to the Mrs.

She did not hear Boggy let himself into the house.

Bob had let him drive that morning. After he dropped his dad at the dairy, instead of parking the truck back home and going to school, he'd kept it and purposely missed the school bus. With the holidays past, deliveries came earlier than they had at first, and Boggy had had a hunch it would be a good day for packages. He wanted to surprise his Kiri. His hunch proved out. He had four parcels, jewels for his beloved. He happily imagined her pleasure as she tore at the brown boxes.

From the door, he heard music. It was Kiri singing a wandering song in Sinhalese. He had never heard her high voice in song. Nor had anyone in America or Kuwait. Ever since she left the sisters with whom she'd practiced many songs, she sang only when she was alone. Boggy held Kiri's treasures in his hand and forgot them as he listened, afraid to make any sound that would betray his presence. Discovered, she might stop. The quivery singing might end. The words were not words he had ever heard and the tune seemed to travel like fragrant smoke though the air. He moved quietly toward her in his boyish enchantment, wanting her to go on and on until the smoke wrapped him round and he was full of the scent of it.

There she was on her elbows and knees, singing. Her bottom rocked violently from side to side as she battled with the sticky debris under the stove. Her hair was uncombed and the quarter inch of black that had grown out since she'd bleached her hair the color of lemons fell away here and there, revealing her creamy scalp. Her soggy T-shirt dragged on the floor as if it were weighted. Boggy smelled the sharp mixture of chemical cleansers she liked to use, and he smelled her sweat. Her feet and legs were bare. She had rolled her worn back leggings up to her knees so that the knees rested on a kind of cushion. Then he saw that the rear seam was ripped and her leggings pulled apart, then closed, as she gave herself to her song and her work. Open, he saw the cleft of her bottom, wiry black hair, deepening shadow. He saw, from behind, a rippling pink edged with brown like a nearly raw steak. Open. Close. He watched until he could not breathe without willing himself to do so. He did not know what to do. Gently, he reached his hand out. He could not resist.

Kiri screeched in fury. The sponge hit the wall and her yellow-gloved hand hit his face. Bad!" she spat.

Boggy lost all balance and his back hit the wet floor as the packages flew up into the air. Ashamed and humiliated, he began to cry and could not stop. "I'm sorry. I'm sorry. I'm so sorry." His penis had escaped his trousers. It wobbled red and miserable above his supine body. Boggy groaned and tried to cover himself.

Kiri shoved his hand away and pushed his penis back and forth like the needle on a metronome. "Once more like that and I shall feed you directly to the IRS! You mustn't ever touch. Kiri is very very pure, you know. Kiri is very pure and not to be leaped and crept upon like a beast."

"I am so, so sorry," he whimpered.

Now Kiri giggled. "You brought me packages?"

Boggy nodded. "Four."

"That is a good boy." Kiri wiped her forehead with her shirt, teasing him with a glimpse of her breast. "What shall we do to thank the little fellow?" she asked as she squeezed his penis with her yellow hand and yanked. Boggy pierced his lip with his teeth as he bit down against the pain, and she let her grip loosen. The rubber glove felt strange on him, the chafing stifled his pleasure and the grime of the floor had rubbed off on him. What was that filth? he wondered, closing his eyes, not wanting to see. Kiri removed her glove and stroked him gently and then he felt safe again.

"Will you sing?" he asked.

She nodded. "Because Kiri says you are a very very good boy." Boggy smiled as she began her song and her caresses.

"Oh God, I love you," he said as his eyes closed once more, this time in trusting surrender.

Kiri gasped. "Oh my God," she answered, pulling her hand away. She saw Bob Wickett at the window. She saw his gun. It was pointed at her. Her, and maybe the boy. She did not dare to stand or move or speak.

"Don't stop," Boggy whispered, taking her hand in his own, unaware of the threat. Then his father smashed the glass and a shard skated over Boggy's stomach, cutting a crimson furrow. Now the boy knew. He pulled himself into a ball and wondered if he was going to die fast or slow. Kiri huddled with her head down, biting her knees, knowing an ancient true fear, but this time without the blindness of nostalgia.

"Don't fuckin' move," said Bob. "Either of you."

The Letter

D ear, dear, dear. Why can't you be content with the
miseries Nature wreaks upon you with such uninten-
tional generosity? Why must humankind always seek
more sorrow than it needs? Does a goose remain north to freeze
in the winter? I ask you. Famine, flood, even pestilence are not
enough! No, humankind digs for trouble like truffle pigs dig
for treats, throwing up dirt all around. But let me not digress.

A letter had arrived. It traveled all the way from Colombo
in the country of Sri Lanka, where, like here, trouble abounds.
When it came, I cannot say. My attention was elsewhere and
it was not addressed to me. It had on it, amid a lot of artful
curlicues, the name Sheila Jericault, though the letter was not
for her, either. Mrs. Onthwaite received it at her house on Currier Street. She was miffed that the letter had somehow failed
to be properly forwarded and that she would have to be incon-
venienced, but for a change, I was neither cursed nor blamed.
She faulted the present government. She intended to ring
Sheila and let her know that an odd-looking foreign missive had
arrived, but she was a busy woman. In order to remember the

letter at all, she placed it in her purse. There it gathered pencil smudges and lipstick smears.

Meanwhile, life went on for Sheila as if there were neither a disaster in the Wickett household nor an important letter from abroad.

As time passed, Sheila was happy, actually happi*est,* in Hallerman's arms, and he in hers. However, it had occurred to Sheila that it might be nice to widen the perimeter. She began to entertain the hope, for instance, that they might one day be able to eat dinner together in a restaurant without fear of being spotted, to hold hands in public, and so on. "I feel like a fugitive," she said one afternoon when he had skipped lunch and come to her cottage.

"You and me both," he answered, turning onto his back and closing his eyes.

Sheila thought of Kiri. She had a new and happy life. "Why," she began carefully. "Um, we love each other, right?"

"Right."

"And you are not, technically, legally married, right?"

Hallerman knew where the conversation was going. He had never loved Carol this intensely and he never could. She had been so generous, a refuge, calm waters, a harbor, when battered from love and losing, he had needed cover. She was a blessing who had become a bittersweet debt, but he dared not leave her. Not for love. Never for love. He'd loved two wives. Love was a ticking bomb. He had to get control. "Right."

"So why don't we, uh . . ." Have a baby, she thought, and giggled at the sudden notion of her mother fussing happily over a grandchild. "You know . . ."

Hallerman tried to bargain, with me, with fate, with Carol. Please, a little more, he pleaded. Please a little longer. Please. He would pay. Anything. He promised. He swore it. He reached out and pulled Sheila into his arms. He held her with all his strength and when he kissed her, it was a bitter kiss.

Sheila might have asked why, but she feared the answer. The phone rang, and she gratefully jumped from the bed to answer it. It was Hal Orinsek. "So what's up?" she said cautiously, watching Hallerman search for his socks.

"Our little project," Hal began. "Anything?"

"She's running for president of the PTA."

"This is getting on my nerves."

Sheila rested her cheek on Hallerman's back. "What can I say? Maybe it's time to restrategize."

"I don't know." Hal fished for an explanation. "All this . . . Uh, maybe she's like, covering up, atoning for some major sin or, like, neglecting her boys? Is she pawning off the kids while she saves the world?"

"Wishful thinking, darling. But I'll prod a little, just for you." Hallerman stood and pulled on his pants. Then he grabbed his shirt and thrashed his way into it, cursing and buttoning his buttons furiously. "Oh shit, what is it?" said Sheila.

"What is what?" said Hal. Hallerman said nothing.

"Sorry, Hal. Gotta go. A pot's boiling over." She put down the phone. Hallerman paced and cursed. Sheila watched him. She touched the cold window and then put her hand to the glass. "Daffodils," she commented. "They're ready to pop." Hallerman checked his watch. "I hate your watch."

"I hate this situation as much as you."

"No you don't," said Sheila. Suddenly, she wondered if, when he went home, he showered and washed off any scent of her, if he scrubbed and scrubbed until he was clean. Sheila placed her chilled hand on his face and looked in his violet eyes. No solutions there, just two small wild, sparkling seas, just beauty and rage, equally untouchable. Hallerman took her hand and they walked to the doorway. No matter who hated what, it was time to go.

Violently, they came together, bracing against the portals, and when it was over, both were bruised and neither was satisfied and they laughed for some reason other than joy.

Sheila walked Hallerman to his Jeep in her bare feet. The spring mud was cold and the wind made her toes sting and burn. "Get back inside," he ordered. But she didn't want to. She watched him go and stood there defiantly taking the pain and not knowing why. When she was finally ready to give in, she hobbled into the cottage, poured herself a sherry, and made a three-log fire. She sat by the flames calling herself an idiot, rubbing her red feet out of numbness, coaxing them past hot agony to a rather pleasant tingling and then to simple warmth.

It was precisely at that moment that Mrs. Onthwaite dumped her purse on her kitchen table while searching for her pince-nez. She found them and placed them over her nose, delighted that she could see. She also found the letter with the lovely Sri Lankan stamp and decided to do something about it before the damned thing got buried a second time.

Sheila Drove Almost Recklessly

S heila drove almost recklessly from the Onthwaite house to Dahlia's. What kept her from running red lights and stop signs was this: Six months after her own writing in Kiri's words, she had in her hand a letter in response and she wanted to live to learn the contents. That Kiri had told a false story in her letter and that it had troubled Sheila to mail these lies made her no less eager. She felt such curiosity about the answer. She was barely able to resist an early peek.

She parked at a meter and hurried to Dahlia's Nails, running up the two flights of stairs. "Kiri!" she called as she opened the glass door, and then, "Kathy," as she remembered the name that Kiri had taken for her work. She glanced at Kiri's table. Everything was in its place. But there was another girl in her seat. Sheila approached the reception desk. "Doesn't Kathy work today?"

"She did," came the answer. "But she is no longer with our employ."

"Oh?" Sheila was startled. "Why?"

"Uh . . ." The receptionist had not expected "Why?"

"Is she ill? Was she fired? Did she quit?"

The receptionist hesitated. "She just didn't come. She stopped coming was all. She . . . I . . . I have her pay envelope here from last week, and I don't know."

"Was there anything wrong?"

"Not that I know. Not here. But . . ."

"Did you call her at home?"

"Elaine did."

"And?"

The receptionist scratched her right palm as if the itch were intolerable. She looked at the red stripes her nails had drawn over the inside of her hand. "Kathy told me you were her friend."

"I am," said Sheila. "Maybe her best friend."

The receptionist stood and leaned across the appointment book. Sheila bent forward so that the woman's lips could meet her ear. "He told Elaine, he said, 'If I ever see that foreign whore again, it'll be too soon.' His exact words. And he slammed the phone right down on Elaine without even saying 'bye or nothing. So I don't want to mail her money to his house, 'cause how will I ever know if she got it?"

"Do you think she's all right?"

The receptionist rubbed her hands over her eyes as if to clear them. "I can't say. She never had a bad word . . . but you know. They could've had a fight, right? The way guys are. But she'll call soon or something, right? I mean, she wouldn't walk away from her pay, right?"

"I don't think she would."

"She's probably just fine. She'll probably turn right up the minute you walk out the door. Don't you think?"

"Yeah," said Sheila, but she didn't mean it. Kiri was gone. "Damn." Sheila ran down the stairs faster than she ran up them. Thinking of Bob Wickett and his gun and his fury, she drove straight to Applewood, damning the Good Deed she'd done and her hurry to be done with it; she sped there, half hoping the police would follow.

She rapped on the Wicketts' door. She had not thought of what she might say, and now fear left her blank. Bob Wickett saw her and nodded once. Sheila let herself in. Bob did not smile or stand to greet her, but he did not tell her to get lost. Her eyes searched the room for his gun. She did not see it. He might have it in his pocket. He might have it in his hand. It might be behind him, tucked under a throw pillow. "Beer?" he asked, picking up his own.

"Thanks," said Sheila, waiting for her host to rise.

"In the fridge."

"Thanks," she said again, making her way to the kitchen. She pulled open the Frigidaire and knew Kiri had not been there for some time. She would never have tolerated crusty milk spills and the smell of spoiling take-out food. Bob heard her pop the top of her Michelob and called out, "If you don't mind, I'll have another." Sheila took one from the refrigerator, handed Bob his, and forced a smile as she sat beside him on the couch.

"So," she began cheerfully. "How you been?" Bob didn't answer. Sheila took a sip of her beer and then another as if no answer were the usual thing. Looking at her shoes, she noticed Bob's gun was right in front of her, on top of the *Reader's Digest* on the lower shelf of the coffee table. Somehow, that reassured her, knowing where it was. "How 'bout you, Boggy? How *you* been?"

Sunk so deep inside the flowered armchair that the cushion curled up around his thighs, Boggy was almost invisible. Sheila was afraid that if she leaned forward to see his face and moved too close to the weapon, someone might grab it and use it. So all Sheila could see of the boy was his greasy jeans and his dirty fingers reaching, at intervals, into the bucket of Kentucky Fried Chicken that sat on his knees. "Totally suckoid," he said.

"Cut the language," snapped Bob. "Boggy's been going through a little problematical stage. He's just fine."

"Thanks, Dad," Boggy drawled. "Good thing I got you for telling everybody how I been or I might not've known." Boggy put on a fake chipper voice. "I been great! Never better! And howsabout you?"

Sheila winced. "Kind of good. I got a little . . ." She sensed it wasn't time to ask. She reached for her beer and leaned on the arm of the couch to get a real look at Bob. He sat as if the pain from the shot and the surgery was gone, but he looked ill. "How's the recovery, Bob?"

Bob folded his hands together. "Coming. But you ought to want to know we had some real trouble here with your colored girl."

"*Dad*," Boggy whined. The boy's knees were jiggling. The cardboard bucket bounced. Sheila waited for it to hit the floor but it didn't.

Bob ignored his son. "Had to let her go, sorry to say."

"That's a lie," said Boggy, quietly, bitterly.

"What is?" asked Sheila.

"He's about as sorry as . . ." Boggy couldn't think of what his dad was sorry as. "Sorry as shit," he said at last.

"Watch yourself," Bob snarled.

Boggy leaned forward and pushed the gun off the magazine in the direction of his father. "What? You gonna shoot me if I don't, Dad? Go ahead. Blow me away. You're not sorry."

This time Bob didn't argue or threaten. The hatred in his son's voice was unmistakable. "Nope. I'm not even slightly sorry, Boggy. She was no good." Bob looked at Sheila. His eyes were reddened as if the salt tears he refused to cry had burned the whites. "She was bad, Boggy." He loved that boy and he did not know if the boy would ever love him back the way he always had. "I explained," he said. "You gotta take my word. Twisted. She was . . . Man, I wish I never laid eyes . . . You can't tell a kid at his age what he don't want to hear. They're experts. . . ."

"Right, Dad," said Boggy. "You got the gun, so you're right."

Bob pretended that was a joke. "He's got this thing about the gun."

Sheila stood so she could see Boggy's face. "You want to tell me what happened?"

Boggy looked away. "I can't."

"I won't get anyone in trouble," she promised.

"I can't."

"Wasn't what you'd call pretty," said Bob, as if to back up the boy's reluctance.

"Did you shoot her?" Sheila had not intended to be so blunt. Boggy glared at his father.

"No," said Bob. "But . . ."

"But?"

"Not 'cause I didn't want to."

Sheila believed him. "So then, where is she?"

"Damn good thing I don't know."

"I need to find her," said Sheila. "So if you hear . . ." Sheila reached in her purse and found a pen. She tore a page from her calendar. As she wrote out her number, she said it aloud very slowly so that if what she was writing was destroyed, Boggy might remember. She handed Boggy the page. He folded it and folded it and folded it, smoothing each crease defiantly. He leaned forward, grinning as he handed the bucket of chicken to his dad, and then he retreated behind the wings of the chair. He arched his back and shoved the small paper lozenge deep down his front pocket.

"You better not," warned Bob.

Sheila Was So Relieved

S heila was so relieved that Hallerman was on his way. He was coming, her lifesaver, just when she needed him. They'd scheduled this four hours the week before. And wasn't that pure luck? He'll know what to do about Kiri, thought Sheila. She would tell him the whole story, what she knew of it, up to the last half hour, and he would help her. She checked the kitchen clock. He was due at ten, and it was ten after. Sheila freshened her perfume and ground coffee beans. She was too distressed to bother with more. He'd love her without her mascara. He'd love her if she didn't light a fire. Sheila sat in the corner of her couch with her knees up. She planned to sit there until Hallerman came. What else could she do? Kiri was missing, gone off into the atmosphere without a word, much less a passport, and it was her fault. It had been so easy to free a slave. Now the fuck what? she wanted to know.

The phone rang. She knew it would be Hallerman, not wanting her to worry. She ran to it. "I need you!" she cried.

"Carol's mother is here." His words were barely audible. "Can you hear me?"

"Not really."

"Her mother. A surprise visit."

"Her mother?" That made no sense to Sheila. "So?"

"Her *mother*." His voice was saturated with frustration.

"This is urgent, honey," Sheila whispered, as if she, too, were constrained from speaking normally. "I *need* you."

"I know," he said wearily, not knowing at all.

"Can't you just go out for an hour? I mean, if it's a surprise visit, I mean . . . Couldn't you . . . Don't you . . . already have plans?"

"Can't." Now he was resigned. "I got roped into looking at fixtures."

"Fixtures!" Sheila shouted. "I'm talking life and death. A missing person."

There was a silence and then a long sigh. "Carol and I are remodeling the kitchen."

Sheila looked up and saw nothing. Her tears had blinded her. Who was she crying for now? she wondered. "The kitchen?" When Sheila thought of Hallerman, when they were apart and she wanted to see him in a place, she did not imagine him at the hospital, masked and gloved, but in that kitchen, dusty with flour, making those magnificent oysters. "Remodeling the kitchen?" And who was going to help her now? Hallerman was looking at fixtures. She was alone. "I . . ." There were so many words that came after I, Sheila didn't know which to say first. This she did know: Her words wouldn't matter.

"I have to go, my love," he said sadly.

Carol's mother. Carol's kitchen. "It's really urgent. Is there any way at all . . ."

"No thanks." His voice altered once more. It was suddenly, heartlessly crisp. "We already subscribe." And then there was no sound at all, a dead line, nothing. Sheila held the phone in her hand, unable to end even the nothing until a torturous *deet-deet-deet-deet-deet* forced her to put the receiver back in its cradle. The kettle screeched. She let it. Her mouth had gone sour. Sheila understood everything about him now, about him and her—if not everything, all the true things. Her throat burned as if she'd nibbled the leaf of a poisonous plant. She'd seen the plant and picked the pretty leaf, wanting nothing but to taste it, no, devour it. She'd placed it between her lips with loving fingers and willed it to have a sweet taste. It had. Until it hadn't, the pretty poison leaf. It had always been what it was. Still, she had willed and wished and wanted, and she was shocked at the fiery pain.

So what? she thought, I'll live.

Sheila made coffee for herself. The making calmed her some. She steamed the milk as slowly and perfectly for herself as she would have done for her lover. Kiri was missing. Hallerman was gone. Poor Hallerman, she thought tenderly. He'd tuck his heart and all its secrets into an airtight jar with a rubber seal and stick it way up in one of his remodeled kitchen cabinets, way up and at the back where nobody except maybe a child could reach, and there it would stay. She knew it. There was no point in wishing otherwise unless just for wishing's sake. She set her cup on a saucer, and the saucer on a table, thinking it funny that she knew Hallerman's fate and not her own. She stared out the window at the radiant forsythia, not minding the mystery quite as much as she thought she ought to do. Earlier that week, there had been only a tentative green; now all the buds had broken open. Not early. Not late. In their own time. There was a wall of new yellow flowers hiding the ancient stone wall that divided the grass from the road, so that even the gray unliving rock had its part, as a host to life. She sensed that if she went outside, if she breathed the air in as far as it would go, the ache of freshness would give her relief, and it did, spring air being a most gentle balm.

Serendipity

Sheila deliberately kept the letter from Sri Lanka (which in times before was also known as Serendip, the resplendent land where, if you tire of the Jewish and Christian legends and fancy the Muslim tale, Adam and Eve were able to console themselves after the cherubim and the flaming sword barred any return to Eden) centered at eye level on the mantel above the fireplace. She put it where she would have to see it several times daily so that she would not fail to wonder and seek until the day she knew and found.

Sheila feared that Kiri was dead—that, more exactly, she had been killed—and faulted herself for ever having let her go. Sheila had believed Bob Wickett when he said he did not shoot her, but as the days passed without word, she asked herself if her belief had simply been a comforting convenience, an easy way out. She doubted herself. She doubted Bob. And she began to either recall or imagine the scent of gun powder in his living room. She did not know which.

The truth was that if she smelled gun powder, it was not the aftermath of murder. Not only was Miss Kiri Srinvasar wholly alive in body and so on, as the result of a serindipitous trip to the mall that had led to a table shared with a kind and helpful woman who said, "Call me Mary," Kiri found herself in the midst of what she considered to be the worthiest and most delighting of employments, one that required neither passport nor papers and yet satisfied as if custom-made to her measure while rewarding her daily with great sums of money. Kiri slept in greater luxury than even the Marriott had offered and though there was no warm pool of still water at her new home and she still lacked a golden card embossed with her own name, she was as close to content as she had ever imagined she might be while confined by mere humanity to the smelly world of men. And Kiri could be patient knowing beyond doubt that the magnificent future would be very shortly the magnificent and eternal now. That was almost enough.

Kiri's Earthly Paradise

Kiri's earthly paradise was known to those who knew of such things as The Willow Retreat, and it is very unlikely that Sheila Jericault would ever, *ever*, have found her there on her own.

Kiri rose every morning at four, just as she had done when she was in service to the Mrs. Only now she rose out of soft pink sheets. Before morning coffee, she showered and painted her eyes, forehead, and cheeks to resemble an elaborate and exotic mask of joyful cruelty. After coffee and pleasant chatter with the other girls, she laced herself loosely into a black stretch vinyl corselet and brushed her teeth and painted her lips and nails a savage red. She then fastened her black fishnet stockings to her leather garter and slid into her shoes, also black, and possessed of heels that could and did double as weapons. Dressed and ready, she consulted the schedule book to see who the early-morning naughty boys might be. It mattered. They each had their own treasured punishment, and Kiri, known to them as the Goddess, took her pay and pleasure making sure they got it. To her, it was a slave's dream come true, to dominate the master. How right, how proper, she thought. Kiri made sure these naughty boys suffered as she had suffered, saw them weep and whimper. She refused them. Punished them. Whipped them with switches. She demanded their worship and thanked them with more cruelty. In exchange, they left The Willow Retreat happily humiliated and, having paid hundreds of dollars for their disgrace, returned, relaxed and eager, to their positions of power in the world that Kiri could not legally enter.

During the lull of off-hours, the Goddess and her Willow sisters, for that is what they called one another, laughed as they watched for the faces of their naughty boys on TV, on the news, in the soap operas. They were often to be found there.

Though many a god, including myself, acts without reason or motive, at least from your point of view, I am not mentioning this idleness idly. Have you guessed? Yes. Kip Coxx was among them. Having given up common philandering for the sake of his career and repented right and left for sins committed and un-, he had turned wholeheartedly to accepting his punishment. Nowadays, he favored a severe paddling by his angry Ballet Mistress (usually Mary), who could not forgive him for soiling the pink tulle tutu he wore over his bare and hairy bottom. He would weep and then masturbate into a hundred-dollar bill. His trips to The Willow Retreat seemed to still his other urges, and Hal Orinsek, who assumed Kip's interest in ballet was of a more conventional nature, knew nothing of this. He felt Kip was coming along almost perfectly in spite of Polly Coxx's ever-expanding list of virtuous deeds. Kip assumed his secret was secret and belonged to him alone, forgetting that on the other end of the paddle stood a human being with the usual assortment of human traits.

Meanwhile, to our present tale. One pearl pink morning when Kiri had finished with her predawn naughty boys and had none scheduled until dinner, she tried to pull on her blue jeans.

She could no longer zip them. Ah, the blessing, she thought. It was becoming outwardly apparent. She squeezed into leggings and a big pink sweater that covered her tummy and telephoned for a taxi.

The Farbury Mall

W hile Kiri made a daily fortune punishing the naughty boys, Sheila worried. She started spending two evenings a week, with or without Polly, serving dinner at the soup kitchen in the basement of the Farbury Congregational Church, often alongside a handsome Englishman, a carpenter named Joshua Levine, whose name I do not mention accidentally. Ladling soup and slicing chicken took her mind off Hallerman. Serving pie and hot coffee took her mind off herself, and she found that tending to needs other than her own was more gratifying than she ever would have guessed. And though with his ready laughter, the recently divorced Mr. Levine was himself a very promising distraction—which is the beginning of another story, the one I am not telling, the one in which in a year or so he becomes her first husband and they live well and happily for a long-enough time—Sheila was too busy thinking about the fate of Miss Kiri Srinvasar to notice who Joshua Levine might turn out to be. And that was as it should be. Chatting with the old, the poor, the wanderers, and the sick gave her an opportunity to put the word out in case one of the other misplaced or displaced should happen upon any news. Sheila could not convince herself that it was time to call in the police. Her new friends concurred. It was Elaine at Dahlia's who suggested she check the Farbury Mall. "She *loved* stuff," said Elaine. "Look there." It was a good suggestion and Sheila took it. On the wrong day.

On the right day, Boggy was an hour early even though he hated to hang at the Farbury Mall. He didn't love stuff, and that was all there was. Far as he was concerned, he could have skipped the mall for the rest of his life except that it was the only place he could easily sneak a visit with Kiri and not get nailed for it. She was worth it, but every time he went, he ended up feeling hypnotized by the artificial light and all the things set up so that you thought you wanted them, whether you did or not. Boggy didn't want much except a new pair of Nikes. And Kiri. And his dad to be regular and happy like before. But forget about that, he thought. He stared at a window full of costume jewelry. Boggy had eighteen dollars he'd earned help-ing the Marches. He thought about maybe getting Kiri a pres-ent. She liked stuff he couldn't afford. Diamonds and rubies and sapphires. The real ones.

He floated toward a lavender scent and into a store called Bubbles. It was all soaps and powders and oils that smelled like everything except oil, the kind of place he would have gone into on birthdays and Christmas and Mother's Day, if he'd had a mom. He was glad he had Kiri even if she wasn't that. He saw six baskets full of oversized see-through colored soaps. Maybe this, he thought, so when she washed and rubbed that soap all over her body, she would think of him. He decided he would get two the same smell. One for her. One for him. They would think of each other. Boggy busied himself at the baskets, comparing ovals of color and scent. The best color was a red that smelled wrong. There was a yellow, a zippy fresh lemon, and a kind of orange-brown that had a thick spicy aroma. He held the yellow to his nose, inhaled, and then the brown, trying to decide which would be exactly right. Yellow, inhale. Brown, inhale. Yellow, inhale, brown. Finally a saleswoman approached the boy. "Can I help you?"

Boggy blushed. "No." He remembered his manners. "Thanks."

"A gift?"

"Um, yeah. For . . . my girlfriend. And, uh . . ."

The saleswoman took a yellow and a brown into her own hands and held each up to her nose. "I would say that for a girl your age, the nice lemon or even a nice gardenia . . . The patchouli is okay, too, of course. Exotic faraway places, lions and tigers. But maybe a little overwhelming, don't you agree?"

She held out the orange-brown bar to make her point. Boggy inhaled so deeply he got woozy. "Yeah." The patchouli was it. Fierce lions and tigers. Kiri would like that. No nicey-nicey. Boggy bought two, had one boxed and gift wrapped, and hurried to the carousel by the food court.

Kiri was there. "You are late, you bad boy," she chided, giving him a one-armed hug, then shoving him away. He handed her his gift. She smelled the package and he knew he had chosen well. "Ahhh . . ." she sighed happily.

"How're the kids?"

Kiri had not mentioned her satisfying work at The Willow Retreat to Boggy Wickett. Instead, she'd told him in a weary voice that she cared for a family of unruly boys whose parents were rarely home. "Oh. Very usual."

"Good? Bad? What?"

She lifted the soap to her nose once more. "There are no boys as good as Kiri's Boggy. Oh no. You are utterly the best. These are very naughty boys and I must strictly discipline them all the time and still they do not learn."

Even though Kiri said he was the best, Boggy was jealous of these boys. He wanted the details. Did she touch them as she used to touch him? Were they permitted what he had been denied? "Do they um . . . Do you . . . Is, uh, any of them . . . Do they help you with your treasures?"

"No and no no no. I am very very finished with questions."

After they ate pizza, Boggy wandered from store to store at Kiri's side. They stopped to watch a fountain lit with pink, blue, and yellow lights. Kiri leaned forward on the silver railing. "It is like the happy days of my fond first coming to a mall such as this," she said. "We have a very very very beautiful world. I will be sad even whilst I am most joyous to be leaving it."

Boggy was alarmed. "Are you going back to, um, Sri Lanka."

Kiri shook her head quite vigorously. "Ceylon. Like the tea. I am never going back."

"Good."

"I am meaning, of course, that I will be dying right here and not traveling to do so."

Boggy slammed his hand on the railing and bruised it. "You are not going to die! If anybody bothers you, you let me know and I'll blast 'em." Boggy pointed his finger as if it were a gun and made a shooting noise. Then, embarrassed at his childishness, he shoved his hands deep in his pockets. In one, he felt a knot of paper. He pulled it out. It was worn from having been washed a few times, but seeing it, he remembered what it was. "Oh!" he said. He unfolded the paper and smoothed it out. The number, in ballpoint, was pale but readable. "Um, Sheila." He handed her the paper.

"Ah! My dear treasured friend Sheila at last. I telephoned her not so very recently, however, she is not residing where she once was."

"She, um, came to my house. She was looking for you. She had something. I don't know if it was a big deal or what. I, um, didn't say anything to her like about where you were, but she wanted me, if I like saw you or anything, to say call."

"Splendid!" Kiri clapped her hands. "Everything is precisely as perfect as it should very well be."

Boggy didn't see it that way. He was worried about the dying stuff. "Um, you didn't hear from my dad or anything, did you?"

Kiri understood. "Heavens no no no no no. I am speaking most delightedly about the blessing. Kiri is chosen to be having the baby in a very very soon time."

"Sheez." Nobody had ever said anything like that to Boggy Wickett before. Babies were good, so he thought maybe he should congratulate her. But she wasn't married. And who was the dad? That would make a difference, wouldn't it? Maybe he was the dad. He tried to figure it: Maybe somehow when she touched him, his sperm got in, like maybe after if she went to the bathroom and wiped herself? "Sheez, Kiri. I mean, not that . . . Am I? Or maybe . . . You don't have to say, but . . ."

"Goodness me. Naturally it is not a this or that or maybe matter, boy. Kiri is most definitely the undefiled and purest virgin, pure pure pure. No man touches Kiri in the most sacred place. Oh, never so!" she declared. "Never ever so!"

Don't look to me to dispute her claim. In the past few thousand years, I have heard others like it. And do you think that I have the time to monitor the copulation patterns or absence thereof among the however many billion humans, not to mention wolves, mountain lions, and anteaters, on this one peculiar planet? Most certainly I do. I have, as I have oft mentioned, *all* time. But that does not mean I am inclined to use it in that fashion. And were I, I might reply that whatever my knowledge might be, you are not meant or entitled to have an answer to every question you ask. What would be the fun in that? And so: I do not dispute her claim, nor shall I presently point to it as Truth.

Boggy, however, was sure he knew what was what. "Then you can't possibly be pregnant," he declared. "Maybe you're sick."

Kiri stopped in front of Anderson's Leather and Suede to

admire his-and-her bomber jackets. She squeezed Boggy's shoulder fondly and said, "It *is* a nice casual look, perhaps with a fine-quality satin lining. Come. Never mind about it."

Boggy flicked his hair back out of his eyes. He was glad to never mind about it. What else was he to do? He decided that if by some weird chance Kiri was pregnant and if by some weirder chance the baby was his, he would run away to another state, lie about his age and whatever else he had to lie about, and take her for his bride so that they could be a family. Having made this oath to himself, he took Kiri's hand and followed her into the store.

What It Took

B oggy stayed as long as he could and then rushed back to school in time for his sixth-period math quiz. He didn't have time to put his new leather jacket into his locker, but he wouldn't have anyway. A guy didn't get a jacket like this every day of his life and he wanted to show it off. So he wore it to class. After math, he had questions to answer. Everybody wanted to know how he got so lucky. And Boggy, who had never mentioned Kiri to anyone except me, and even then only whispering into his pillow at night, said, "My dad."

And then a shy girl who talked so rarely that her voice came as a surprise murmured, "Wow. My dad would rather fly to the moon. Forget about it. Not even on Christmas."

Boggy shrugged. He almost cried. "Yeah. He's real great," said the boy, remembering the days and years of the happy life that stopped when his dad survived the shooting.

By three, when Bob Wickett came round to pick Boggy up from school, his simple lie had become a glorious one. Boggy had told, maybe fifteen times in ever-expanding detail, about how it was that his amazing dad saw how hot Boggy looked in the jacket and laughed because he'd once been a boy and understood in a way parents don't and said, "Oh, what the hell," and sprung for the bomber in cash right on the spot. Boggy told his tale joyfully, proudly, until the mere fact of its untruth seemed minuscule, as easily brushed away as a curl of lint.

He waved exuberantly when he saw Bob's pickup. "There's my dad!" he shouted. The sun bounced over the windshield surrounding Bob Wickett's face in light. "Gotta go!" He ran to the truck and leaped in beside his father. "Hi, Dad!" he shouted, waving to his friends as if in proof.

Bob saw the smile on his boy's face. Boggy was smiling at him, and he offered his thanks to me, Bob did, though I had nothing to do with it. "So'd you ace the test?" he said in just the same easy way he'd always used to say it, glancing sideways cautiously, hoping the smile would stick.

It stuck. "What if I did?"

Bob rejoiced. "I'm starved."

"Me, too." Boggy rolled down the window. The wind pushed at his leather sleeve but couldn't pierce it. "Want to hit Burger King, Dad? Or Mac's?"

"Yeah," said Bob. That was exactly what he wanted to do, but he was too shy with happiness, too afraid to mess up a good feeling, unexpected as it was, and he didn't want to say the wrong thing. That's why he didn't ask about the jacket. At least not right away. "Let's do the King. What do you want to have?"

"Two shakes."

"Pure chemicals."

"Good chemicals. What do I care, long as they taste like chocolate."

Bob laughed. "Preservatives."

"So they'll preserve me and I'll live forever," said Boggy, laughing too.

"Wiseacre." Bob pulled into the parking lot. He was feeling so much that he didn't curse, barely noticed, the driver who stole his space. What does it matter? he thought. I've got my boy.

"Let's take to-go, Dad, and go for a ride," said Boggy. So Bob didn't bother to park at all. They gave their order at the drive-in window. Boggy divvied up the Whoppers and the fries. On the floor, between his sneakers, he braced the flimsy carry-all that held his dad's Coke and his two chocolate shakes.

Bob headed up along Route 8 past the big car dealerships in the direction of the ratty fields and rotting barns. He drove to the sound of chewing. Everything tasted good. They didn't need to talk. Boggy handed him his Coke and started sucking his first shake up through a straw. Boggy sucked so hard, the straw collapsed. "Damn things," he said.

"They make 'em too thick," Bob agreed.

"Yeah, practically solid. And the straw's too thin."

"Yeah." Then Bob took a chance. "Nice jacket," he said tentatively.

"Thanks," said Boggy.

"Real leather."

"Yeah."

"Nice. Kind of a motorcycle jacket."

"Bomber." Boggy stared out the side window, waiting for the rest and wishing there would be no rest, that his lie was true, that his dad would just leave it alone.

"So where'd you get it?"

"Borrowed it," said Boggy. "From a friend. A friend lent it to me."

"Nice friend," drawled Bob as he felt the rage crawl in. His boy. Even his boy couldn't be trusted. "He just lent it. Nice. Let you borrow it."

"Well, actually, no," said Boggy. "It was kind of a present."

"Some present." Bob thought of Boggy's unforgiving sullen ways over the past many months and wondered if maybe it wasn't all that foreign bitch's fault for ruining the kid. Maybe there was more. "Uh . . . This friend, uh, involved with, uh, drugs?"

Boggy glared at his father. "Nobody can be just nice, right? You think I can't, like, maybe have a real friend who really *likes* me, like maybe wants to give me something for a present, right? No. You always think there has to be something bad about everything."

"That's not what I'm saying," said Bob. "Not at all." But it was what he thought.

"Yeah, sure, Dad. You're just, like, bringing up drugs out of the blue, huh?"

Bob put his foot to the gas to beat a light and kept going fast.

"You used to know me. You would have never used to ask me something like that. You used to trust me. Now you hate everybody. That fucking gun. Just 'cause you got shot, Dad. It's not everybody's fault. I'm sick of it. Sick of it. It's not my fault!"

That fucking gun, thought Boggy. Suddenly Boggy knew what to do. He lunged for his dad's ankle holster. He grabbed the gun. Then he winged it out the window as hard as he could.

"God damn you! My gun!" Bob spat. He slammed the brakes with both feet. The truck responded with a savage jerk. Boggy flew through the windshield at fifty-eight miles per hour.

And I intervened. There are those of you who make much of my legendary compassion. Let us leave distracting legends aside. I had my reasons. But I might have done it even if I hadn't.

Or not, as you have often and sadly observed.

So this was the tragedy avoided: splitting his skull as his head hit the black pavement and dying in an instant, surrounded by his brains.

And this, the opportunity, the chance: In a ruby rain of blood and glass, he flew, landing in a shallow bog thick with soft weeds and black spring mud, breaking both his legs, both his arms, and two ribs.

Bob ran to his boy, holding Boggy's body with all his strength. He did what he could, which wasn't much, pressing his hand at Boggy's forehead where the blood coursed out and filled his eyes. Bloody-handed and bloody-faced, rent by grief, Bob howled a red cry. "Not him! Not Boggy! Take me!" he begged and screamed at the sky. "Take me!"

But the sky was tranquil and the sky was silent, as it ever was and shall be. And that was good. For in the silence, Bob Wickett saw himself as his young son had seen him, raging, hate-filled, strangled by obsession. The gun. Every day, all the time, the gun and revenge, revenge and the gun. He knew that though he lived and breathed, he had nothing if he did not have his Boggy, if he lost him now. He saw his future and saw hell, a life of hate, hating the gun, hating himself, hating his hate without rest or forgiveness.

And that is what it took in the particular case of this particularly lucky man.

The hate that had come to define him died instantly. He saw: There was no time for it. No room for it. It was worse than the insult he had suffered and worse than the wound to his body.

Boggy opened his eyes. He was alive. Bob kissed his torn face. A miracle! Life! That was the only thing. Life and his beloved boy. And these two things I granted him. Both, for a very long time.

As I say, I had my reasons. You may never know them.

Because of the Stretch

Because of the stretch, Kiri had had little trouble lacing her rubber corselet. Rubber made generous adjustments. Nothing showed, or nothing that might not be explained another way. Black, Kiri found, was a fine camouflage. The secret was easy to keep.

Then, all of a sudden, or so it seemed, her belly had become an overlarge coconut and the corselet could no longer hold it in. Nothing in her drawers and nothing in her closet could flatten her. The baby growing in her body could no longer be hidden. No secrets anymore, she thought as she glanced through her bedroom curtains and saw a gray Lexus start down the back exit road. Soon it disappeared into the forest. That would mean Mistress Mary's ten o'clock naughty boy had finished. She would be coming up for a snack.

Mary started talking as she climbed the steps, certain there would be someone to hear her complaint. It didn't matter who. She just wanted to be heard. "That fuckin' Coxxie. I never seen anything like it. I mean, I don't mind the fuckin' tutu. I seen plenty of tutu types. But hundred-dollar bills? He fucking beats off into fuckin' hundreds. Sick. Good money wasted on some perv politician. It's sickening. And don't think I wouldn't wash it off, either. Money is money. But no. *He's* got to flush 'em down the goddamn toilet. Hundreds down the john. And you wonder why this country's a mess. He oughta get his head examined. Fuckin' sick. And on top of it all, he's a damn lousy tipper."

Kiri threw a loose shirt over her shoulders, leaving her arms outside the sleeves, buttoning only the button between her weighted breasts. She wandered into the kitchen. "I am having the baby," she announced.

"What baby?" Mary stopped her chatter and stared. "Shit," she said. "Pretty far along, too."

"I am most truly far along with it," Kiri answered.

"I had no fuckin' idea."

Kiri nodded up and down quite sympathetically. "It was, I think, waiting until this very special day to show how it was appearing."

Mistress Mary's face turned grave. "I'd say you gotta be at least . . . how many months there? If you'd have told me, I could have helped you get rid of it."

"My heavens and goodness no no no no no!" said Kiri. "This is not a baby that is for getting rid. This is the Buddha for the new time. We are most blessed."

Mary sat beside the dark-skinned woman and took her hand, stroking it gently. "Does Ann know?"

"To this moment, the Head Mistress has remained in ignorance for it is only from now that the disguising of my miraculous wonder was not entirely possible. Now I propose that I should be telling her."

"She's gonna fire you. No doubt about that," said Mary. "We may have a couple of guys who get spanked by angry mothers, but pregnancy is another kettle of fish. I don't think so. She's definitely gonna fire you."

"Do you tell me that she who has been most kind would truly refuse to shelter the mother of the emerging Bodhisattva at the time of the last birth?"

Mary had no idea what Kiri was jabbering about. "Alls I can say is Ann hates babies and she won't stand the noise around here, no matter what." Mary had had four abortions without tears, but now she wanted to weep in mourning for those who were never born. "I'd like to be an auntie or something if you don't mind. Buy him toys and stuff."

Kiri took her hand. "You shall be a very fine auntie and shall join with my very own dear and natural sisters in this honored post."

Mary hugged her. "You're a pal. What's your money situation? I'll help you if you need."

Kiri's money situation was enviable, but she did need help. Mary took Kiri to a fence who converted all but her favorite jewels to cash and then directly to her own stockbroker, who was able to invest the cash in mutual funds, as a gift to Miss Sheila Jericault. At Kiri's insistence, Mary also helped with the writing of a will containing all her wishes for the future time when she would no longer be in the world of men. And Mary made sure that it was properly witnessed. All the girls at The Willow Retreat read it and signed it in the presence of a favored client who happened to practice law, and then when the client was gone, they put aside the will and threw a baby shower.

"I shall assure you that my son will know in all the details of your most very very wonderful generous offerings to the comfort of his new life, and he will remember his Willow aunties well when he is small and when he is great," she promised, and then as a sign of her own love and appreciation, she removed her pearl bracelet. With scissors, she cut the pearls loose, giving one to each of her new sisters and keeping one for herself.

One Morning When Sheila Could Bear It No Longer

O ne morning when Sheila could bear it no longer, she opened the letter on her mantelpiece. She had contemplated this act over and over, but had resisted, sometimes because it was wrong and sometimes because, even though she knew she was being totally illogical, she feared that somehow the letter might magically contain the words that would tell her conclusively that what she dreaded was true. Her hopes were already as weak as a poor man's broth, but they were all she had left of Kiri Srinvasar, who seemed to be lost forever. She set a kettle on the stove and steamed away the glue. It has come to this, she thought. Even bad news would be welcome. And she swore that she would do whatever it was she had to do next, however unpleasant it might be. She had freed this slave, altered her fate, loosed her on a country that had no place for her, and so she was bound to her, heart and soul, and would never be free nor detached from her destiny. The envelope opened easily. Feeling like a felon, she opened the onionskin stationery, which was folded in thirds. Then before she looked at the writing, she said a small prayer out loud.

"Please let Kiri be safe." Then she looked down at what was written and laughed. "I knew it. What was I thinking?" She laughed helplessly, laughed in despair, laughed and laughed. "Serves me right." The five-page letter certainly contained a great amount of news, but every word of it was in Sinhalese and totally unreadable to her.

She was laughing when the phone rang and laughing when she answered. "Hello?" she wheezed.

"Ah! Yes yes yes, Sheila," Kiri replied. "I am telephoning to you at long last!"

Sheila was silent for a moment. "Oh my God," she said. "You're alive."

"I am most highly alive for this time being," Kiri declared.

Sheila laughed again. This time, in relief. "I have a surprise for you."

"And I, for you. I should very much be delighted to exchange surprises."

"Yes! Where are you? Are you free?"

"I am utterly free," said Kiri.

"Do you want to come now?" Sheila did not want to risk losing her again.

"Certainly."

"Tell me exactly where you are and I'll jump in the car."

"No no no no no. That is not to the slightest measure in any way to be necessary. You must just tell me the where of you and I shall arrive directly for a visit."

"You're sure?"

"More than sure," said Kiri.

Sheila gave her careful directions to the where of her and then, she waited what seemed like an ever-long time. Her throat was dry, but she hadn't the mind to pour a drink. Her hands were cold, so she tucked them under her arms and pulled her knees up to the aching scar on her stomach. And then, at once, she forgot all her fear as a station wagon with darkened windows at the sides pulled up beside the cottage. Sheila ran to the car and pulled open the door. She put her arms around Kiri. Kiri's tears fell upon her cheek, and hers upon Kiri's until at last they had to break apart to dry their faces. The driver helped Kiri out of the car as if she were fragile. He carried two matching leather suitcases into the house and then returned for a brass-trimmed steamer trunk.

"I should have guessed," said Sheila.

Kiri offered the driver a twenty-dollar bill. He refused it, patting her hand. "You hang on to that," he said. "And drink lots of milk."

Seeing Sheila's puzzlement, Kiri explained. "I am having the baby."

"Oh my God." She stared at Kiri's belly, wondering how she had failed to notice on her own. But, as you know, one rarely sees when one is not looking. "How soon?"

"In a very soon time."

"Oh my God," Sheila repeated, invoking my name more times that day than she had done in any day since my interest in her and the business of her soul had been piqued. "Oh. My. God." Then she turned to earthly matters. "Who's the father? Is it Wickett? It's my fault. I'll kill him. Is that why you left?"

"Heavens no! It is most absolutely not any Wickett at all. Kiri's baby cannot have a father because I tell you most assuredly that I remain most totally unentered by any man."

Sheila sighed. "Kiri," she said patiently. "There has to be a father. You can tell me. We don't have to even deal with him if you don't want. I'll help you. We can handle this on our own. But I'd like to know."

"And I shall tell you. Kiri's baby was made in its wholeness through a most lucky and perfect dream. I swam in a pool as much warm as our beloved Marriott pool, but smaller and out of doors. I swam and was not wet. Everywhere at once, lotus flowers popped their bloom. Everywhere there were suddenly full flowers, lotus, all of them. On the water. Under my head for a pillow. The smell of many flowers soaked the air and it lay upon my body like a blanket. The bright sun made me blind and hot. I could not see in this sacred place and yet I saw without my eyes as the baby entered my womb that there was no man the father at all. It is a god child."

Sheila wasn't going to argue. Not then. For some time she had had no reason to recall Kiri's odd and upsetting relationship to what others might call the truth. Now the memory returned. "Are you hungry?"

"Very hungry," said Kiri, folding her hands right over left and resting them on her belly. "My baby is a hungry one. He must grow to a great strength."

Sheila made scrambled eggs and sausages and French toast with maple syrup. Kiri sat quietly as she cooked. After they had eaten, Sheila said, "I have a confession. You know that letter you wrote? Well, an answer finally came. I went over to Currier to pick it up, but when I called Dahlia's they said you left. They were actually incredibly worried because you never picked up your last week's pay. And then, I got hold of Bob Wickett, but he . . . I gave Boggy my number, not him . . ."

"Yes yes. This I know. For it was he who like a very good boy gave his Kiri the number I was able to telephone in finding you."

"I wasn't even sure you were alive. That's why I finally opened it. I'm really very sorry."

Kiri opened her black eyes wide. "And so?" she said, ignoring the apology. "What did it say?"

Sheila shrugged. "I couldn't read a word of it."

Kiri laughed with unbounded pleasure. Sheila handed her the onionskin pages. Kiri read the letter slowly. When she finished, she read it through again. Then she folded the sheets gently and slid them back into the envelope. "It is from my mother's sister, who until she received my letter and the five hundred dollars from America thought I was indeed the most ungrateful and dreadful niece to be imagined. She has written that my mother and my sisters are all dead for nearly five years past. Killed in violence by the Tamil Tigers and dead." Kiri did not cry. She sat silently, ten fingers spread across her face. Sheila sat beside her, a mirror to her silence, captured in it until Kiri chose again to speak. "It is as well. For after the new life begins, we shall be together as I planned, however quite in another place than first I had put in my mind. That is all." She rested her head on Sheila's shoulder, humming as Sheila stroked her hair, and contemplated life after life with bitter-sweet pleasure.

From My Point of View

T hough I will soon have said all I mean to say on the subject of Sheila Jericault and the progress of her soul, from my point of view, I present you not with an end but with one more beginning on one small planet in a glittering gaseous universe among so many other universes, filled with goods and gods and endless beginnings.

Make of it what you will. How you see what you see is up to you. It is not my province.

At any rate, Sheila found Kiri an easier companion the second time round. They were busy. Babies don't wait. Kiri hadn't the time to watch quite so many shopping shows. Better still, during her days at The Willow Retreat, she had developed a taste for the news. One night, as they sat together on the couch consuming a quart of Rocky Road ice cream, an earnest Kip Coxx appeared on the tube.

"Up goes the old phoenix," muttered Sheila.

Kiri wrinkled her nose and sniffed as if at a bad smell. "You do not know Coxxie! He is not a friend, I am hoping?"

"Coxxie?" Sheila smiled and crunched a nut. "Do you know Coxxie?"

"Well, he was a naughty boy. A tutu man with shallow pockets. The worst sort."

"Ah," said Sheila. "Really? You must tell me the whole story."

And she did. And when that story was told, Sheila embraced her, for Kiri had just provided the ammunition Polly and her boys would need to remain unharmed by Hal Orinsek's political schemes.

There were many other things to say and what seemed like endless more to do. Each day, Kiri spoke many times of the elaborate entwinement of her son's life, his emergence as Buddha himself, her own coming death and rebirth to a magnificent and eternal life among the gods, and Sheila's own solemn honor during her mortal days, which was to raise this divine being to be a splendid and compassionate man worthy of his eminence.

It was a lot for Sheila to swallow, and she didn't swallow it, but she listened, attributing Kiri's talk of destiny and death to her grief at her own great losses. Tenderly, she assured Kiri that American hospitals were the finest in the world. "Look at me," she said. "I should have died."

"Oh goodness no no no. You were not finished living! For how should you have died and lived to raise my boy in the proper way? It would be impossible even in Connecticut and the United States of America to do such a thing. Certainly it is an entirely different matter of which I am speaking," Kiri replied.

"Everything will be just fine. You will raise your own child exactly the way you want. I will make sure," Sheila said over and over many times, "that you have the very best obstetrician at Farbury General." And this she did.

Sheila promised that if Kiri wanted to stay, she would be her sponsor and file all the papers necessary so that Kiri could make a life within the law, even if that took fifteen years to accomplish. Sheila said all she could say to reassure Kiri Srinvasar that her birth would be routine in a safe, sanitary, modern way, but Kiri was not reassured. She was furious. She insisted that Sheila read and understand her will. Everything, even the boy, was going to her.

"It does not matter the hospital, I am telling this to you. Wherever wherever, I will bid farewell as I am due and leave my life within seven days of my son's last birth. Then I shall be re-born to splendor as was also so with the honored Queen Maya!" she shouted. "And you, my dear friend Sheila, as I say and say, it is your gift to begin his life so very very very well that his heart will be made open and strong even in the hardest of days."

So that they might go on to other matters, Sheila finally stopped trying to persuade Kiri. Instead, she humored her, making the promises she was asked to make with confidence she would not need to keep them. This brought the tensions to an end.

Late at night, Sheila often thought about Hallerman, and wondered whether she had erred in knowing her lifesaver as her lover. She decided she had not. It was good to know that he was just and only a man. In her stone cottage, in the silence of the night, even as she wept with the ache of longing, Sheila swore that for as long as she lived, her saved and broken heart would be no morning-glory heart, open only to receive the light, furling shut at the first sign of darkness. She refused to be a coward. She would not let her heart close, even if to keep it open, she had to bear both frost and flame without a shield. For too many years her polished shield had worked too well, protected her too completely, and had it not been torn from her, she knew she would never have dropped it. As it was, she felt naked, knew that naked was what she was. She had a soul but she had no answers and she was not ashamed.

Now what? she asked. And in the silence of the night, she returned to an old and cherished habit. Leaning on her elbow in her bed, she wrote lists of what needed to be done. With the help of Joshua Levine, Sheila and Kiri had already searched for and found a precious hand-carved maple cradle. Sheila's mother, who was on a jaunt to London, airmailed the ideal English pram, with wheels that could ride the rough country roads. Kiri's little boy already had the softest pale blue flannel sheeting waiting to enfold him, and resting atop Sheila's dryer were a dozen fuzzy coveralls, washed and then washed again so that the baby to come, Kiri's coming Buddha, would feel no harshness against his skin. Life would be harsh enough, soon enough. Four teddies, a koala, and a stuffed dalmation waited to be cuddled by tiny hands.

1. Ask Joshua re: dresser, Sheila wrote.

Along with her generous advice, Polly passed along a changing table, but the boy had no diapers for his bottom.

2. Diapers.

They had a little bath that would fit inside the kitchen sink and a special baby soap made of herbs, but Sheila thought her towels too rough for new skin.

3. Towels.

She thought they ought to be bright, colorful towels, with his name embroidered on them, whatever his name would be, so that they would be special, all his own. But what of the name? Kiri said she had already chosen her baby's name, but she would not tell it. She said it was to be her secret until the last, but Sheila only half believed the name was fixed.

4. Name, she wrote. And then:
5. ???

One list became several lists, which expanded in her mind and on Post-its and legal pads and the backs of envelopes. Though Kiri insisted that matters would quite naturally order themselves as they should, Sheila tried to consider everything.

On the night she found herself at number six on a list of Ways to Trust to Luck and Instinct, she forced herself to put her pencil in the night-table drawer and close her eyes. Eventually, she succumbed to sleep and her whirling, listing dreams. Unlike the nights before, when she had tossed in silence, this night she heard a scream. It took a second scream before she realized that the first was not inside her head. "Kiri!" She ran to Kiri, who sat panting and wet, wrapped in wet sheets. "It's okay. It's okay. Your water has broken. It's all good. It's okay," she repeated as she dialed the obstetrician. "It's okay." She undressed Kiri. Shocked at the sight of blood, she sponged the red wetness from between Kiri's legs. She sponged her forehead, her back, and under her arms, and dressed her again, in her most comfortable clothes. "Remember to breathe," she ordered, kneeling at Kiri's feet to put on clean socks and the shoes that matched Kiri's favorite nail polish.

Sheila drove to Farbury General, trying not to swerve as Kiri gripped her leg, piercing it with her red nails as the steady, savage explosions in her back shook her small body. Sheila inhaled with her, exhaled with her, petted her hair, and repeated her promises. "Everything's going to be just fine," she said, "It's going to be okay."

"Yes, my very dear friend," Kiri panted, seizing an instant when there was no pain to offer Sheila a joyful smile. "I am so so so so sure of it!"

Kiri thought there would be time for more words, but as it happened, there was not. Sheila held her hand as she was rolled into the delivery room and held her hand as she labored to push her child through her and into the light. Sheila breathed with her, so that their every breath was drawn the same, and then,

Kiri's breathing became a struggle. A nurse grabbed Sheila's arm and yanked her out the door as she heard the doctor curse. Kiri's heart had stopped. They sliced the newborn from her body, and as the nurse bathed it, as it yelled its first cries of life, they fought to make the baby's mother breathe. After twenty minutes, there was again a trustworthy heartbeat, but what would be left of a brain so long deprived of oxygen, the doctors did not know.

For seven days Kiri lay still, alive. Sheila stayed beside her, kissing her forehead, holding her hands, stroking her face, combing her hair, telling her of the baby's deep black eyes, of its golden skin, of the strange whorl of blond between its eyebrows, telling her a baby needed a mother and that she had to, absolutely had to, live.

But Kiri died, just as she hoped and knew she would. Sheila wondered how she could have known. She wondered what it meant. She did not have time to wonder long. There was a tiny new life to tend to. There were all those promises to keep. Sheila smiled. No matter who this child would be, the mysterious responsibility of raising it was hers, and could be no one else's. Life had been given her once, twice, and now, a third time. At last, she knew what to do with it. Humbled by the child's fragility, astonished by the overwhelming magnitude of her awed tenderness for this newborn old-faced stranger, Sheila lifted the infant from its cradle and took a mother's oath, "I will always love you," she said. Then she named the tiny girl Grace.

Grace. Do you want me to tell you now about the fate and meaning of Grace? To confirm, or deny? Give you an answer once and for all? You know I don't do that sort of thing. Because I am fond of you, I give you what you have had all along: possibility.

Make of it what you will.